MADISON MCMAH

THE SON OF MARA

For the dreamers and the doers.

CHAPTER 1

It was an accident.

I swore it was an accident.

Aunt Esther interrogated me until the sun began to set over the cottage. But, as I told her repeatedly, it was simply an accident.

I mean, what did she expect to happen? I thought the boy had returned to be my friend.

"Were you using any herbs or-or- did you use a new type of potion?" Aunt Esther stuttered. She was still scrambling through her mind for an explanation for what I had done as the dinner chime rang.

"No, I just did it by myself." I shrugged, not understanding why this was a big enough deal to miss dinner.

"You can not have struck a person from fifty yards away!"

Maybe that could be considered a big deal.

CHAPTER 2

THE DAY BEFORE

Cut, and mix, and pour. Cut, and mix, and pour. The rhythmic motions of brewing a sealant had become as habitual as breathing. Once again—very not unusually—the frame of the cottage's front door had chipped to the point of the whole structure becoming more of a flapping barrier between the outside and in. Aunt Esther leaned against its pale green paint to keep the bugs from coming in to nibble away at the dried plants hanging from the wooden ceiling. Despite being in between classes, she couldn't resist the opportunity to pepper me with questions, a sorry attempt to keep me on my toes. Nevertheless, it was my sole opportunity to see—or, well, *understand*, at least—the world beyond the cottage.

"How many bones are in a fairy's wings?" She shot.

"Ten total. Five in each wing," I replied, not even having to watch while stirring the herbs into the brew. I only needed to feel the slightest easing in effort while stirring to know when to start the next step.

She nodded. "What are the types of summoners?"

I yawned. Listing the types of people who could call upon creatures of different realms? I gave a haughty laugh, insulted by how easy she was taking it on me. "Underworld, celestial, nautical, and botanical."

Aunt Esther straightened as I slumped down, resting my head in my hands while pouring in a dollop of honey. Her face hardened as she pondered a tougher question. "How long can a witch go without using their power?"

"Hmm," I pretended to think so she wouldn't wind herself up too much. With taking care of the house and homeschooling me being her sole job—our only income the money my father— her (half) brother sends back—she pushed herself excessively to do the best she could. "A week to a few days depending on the witch's power and skill level. The higher the power, the shorter they can go without using it. To maintain a healthy flow of magic, witches must actively use their power—unless they want to be eaten away by it, of course."

Aunt Esther breathed out a laugh. "If I was a real teacher, you would definitely be my ideal student."

"You *are* a real teacher," I reassured her. "It's quite easy to see from the talent of your pupil." I winked at her, and she twisted her lips to suppress a smile, knowing a parent would tell their child that humbleness is a virtue instead. "But now that you mention going to actual school…"

"Blythe…" She shook her head, dissolving my hopeful attempt. "We've talked about this—"

A sound tore through the wind above the cottage, disrupting her speech. Caws and squawks followed, intertwined with the breaking of tree limbs. Then, finally, a thud to the ground. Aunt Esther and I met one another's eyes for only a moment before hurrying outside, the door swinging on its hinges as if encouraging us to investigate. We weaved through our vegetable garden in our wild meadow of a lawn until reaching the edge of the yard.

Sprawled out on the ground was a creature of golden feathers. Everything from its brilliant talons and striking yellow saffron tail would indicate the bird was a griffin if it were not for its small stature and dull beak.

"Why is a griffapuff in Northern France?" I asked, looking up beyond the canopies of trees that tucked our cottage into the woods.

"I'm not sure." Aunt Esther shook her head, assessing the damage as she pressed on the bleeding gash in its chest. One of the hunting humans must have tried to shoot it down from the air.

"Their flight patterns would never take them this far south." She affirmed my knowledge from one of our lessons on magical creatures just weeks ago. Griffapuffs—a mix between a puffin and a griffin—thrived in the utmost northern countries where they worked in tandem with the Vikings. For one to travel to such a warmer place (in the late summer, no less) was inexplicable.

"Go inside and brew the sealant for anatomical use instead of stationary. You'll need to—" She started, but I was more than prepared to put my knowledge to use.

"Change the ratio of the ingredients. I got it!" I dashed inside while Aunt Esther asked the goddesses to aid her in this process. Witches tended to thrive in one field more than another, and Aunt Esther excelled in healing magic. She always encouraged me to dabble in every branch of witchcraft, though. In times like this, it was helpful that I excelled in all of them, but at sixteen years old, I knew the time was coming when I would have to decide. My father would make sure I did, even if he was a country or continent away. That was just the way things were done.

"A beehive's worth of honey, a beehive's worth of honey," I repeated the recipe for an anatomical sealant, one that was capable of healing living things instead of the effect of shutting a door too harshly, as I rummaged through the house. I reached into the cabinet, where jars of elderberry and thyme clinked against crystalized droplets from the Black Sea. I felt around blindly, maneuvering past the bottled giggles of a gnome until I grabbed the tiny pot of honey— the equivalent of a singular bee's labor.

I scurried back outside to the scene. The blood from the griffapuff's wound had started to seep through the crevices of my aunt's worn hands. I held the disappointing jar of honey out for her to see.

Her face sank. "Are you sure there isn't any tucked in the bottom shelf?" Aunt Esther asked.

"Nope, I checked."

"What about the hallway cupboard?"

"Nope, I checked."

"How about the—"

"Nothing else in the kitchen drawers, herb chest, spice rack, or that funny box you keep under your bed," I finished.

"Blythe! What have I told you about—"

"Sorry, sorry!" I held my hands up defensively, a grin pulling at my lips. "But now we *have* to go."

"You remember last time we went," Aunt Esther looked at me pointedly.

"I know better now! No magic around humans," I nodded confidently. Aunt Esther held her gaze on me, cocking a brow. My shoulders slumped.

"Not even a card trick…," I replied begrudgingly.

"Even though they would just think I'm a *magician*, and we could bring in some extra money, and think of their faces when they see me!"

"Blythe…" Aunt Esther started to sigh, but the griffapuff cried out in pain with its black eyes that were becoming more glassy. She closed her own, taking a heavy breath. "We'll get the honey, and then we'll leave." She swallowed harshly as if reassuring herself too. "The wound will hold long enough with raw honey for now. You—"

"I'll grab your satchel," I called back, already halfway in the house.

Canopies of vivid magentas, blinding yellows, and alluring greens shrouded the marketplace from the beating sun, making it impossible for the heat to dwindle the liveliness of the market. People clamored at a booth where open umbrellas blossomed from the top of the stall, desperate to stay in the luxurious shade after leaving the safety of the canopies . From another booth, spherical, cylindrical, and pod-shaped lamps shined gold and white for your attention—even though it was the middle of the day. There were fruits, and furniture, and cups and candles, and though the items themselves were enchanting, it was their history that lured me in the most. Bows from Milan. Bowls from Japan.

And bowels from cows in where only the most organic grass grew
—they said.

I resisted the urge to slip into the flow of people
perusing each booth. Aunt Esther and I stopped at a teal colored
stall lined with obtuse pots, slender jars, and drawstring bags,
each filled with almost every substance imaginable. As Aunt
Esther tried to haggle the price down for *every jar of honey they
had* with a vendor, a swarm of children dashed across the
cobblestone walkway, clutching swirled lollipops and miniature
creatures. One of the toys—a red dragon—sailed above their
heads in the hands of a tall boy with the most radiant blonde hair I
had ever seen. His blinding teeth twinkled in the sliver of light
that slipped through the canopy as he smiled at something his
friend murmured to him. I could not hear the joke, but I wished I
had been the one to say it when he tossed his head up, sending his
golden locks cascading down the collar of his white blouse. The
most enchanting laugh bounded out of him. It was the babble of a
brook on a summer's day. The excited chirp of birds in the
morning. At that moment, I wished nothing more than to be the
orchestrator of such laughter.

"Once my brother returns home, I can come back with
the full sum," My aunt insisted to the vendor in a pinstripe suit,
who replied with, "I understand, Ms. Seraphin but…"

Their conversation trailed off as I snuck away to the stone ledge the children resided at, licking happily at their candies, clapping hands, or comparing toys. The boy sat in the center of the whirlpool of childhood fun, handing his dragon to a smaller child who lit up with glee at the act of kindness. I walked up to him, feeling the reliable weight of my card deck shift up and down in my boot. *Just for a moment*, I reassured myself. It would take time to pack up all the jars and I would reappear as if I had never left.

"Care for a card trick?" I asked, and though the boy looked at me intrigued, he said nothing. I smiled to myself. *A tough crowd? That won't be a problem.*

I fanned out the deck in front of him, beckoning him to take a card. He pulled one out and studied it, holding it incredibly close to his face to block my view, then slipped it back into the deck. Little did he know the enchanted deck caused a card touched by anyone but the dealer to grow a fraction of the size bigger. Practically unnoticeable and perfect for "guessing" the right card.

I shuffled the deck with a flourish, noticing the tail of a card poking out from the rest. By then, I had drawn a crowd of the boy's friends, all waiting to be entertained. Astounded. I was more than happy to oblige.

"Is this your card?" I revealed the queen of hearts, grinning excessively to hide my anticipation. The boy frowned.

11

"You looked," he scoffed. His friends snickered. I clenched the deck as sour determination festered in my palms.

"Pick again then," I thrust the deck towards him. The boy exchanged glances with his friends and plucked out another card, shielding it against his chest while examining it. He slid the card into the deck, and I snatched it back. This time, I made a display out of the shuffle by tossing it from left hand to right, making it wiggle like a worm in mid-flight, and finally, shuffling it with just one hand. With the other, I reached into my dress pocket and crushed some junifere leaf between my fingers.

"Oh no!" I exclaimed, propelling the hand with crushed junifere to the boy's ear and pretending to swat away a fly. "Sorry about that. Didn't want you getting bit. Anyways..." I shuffled a bit more before I picked the slightly enlarged card from its place. *Eight of clubs.*

I beamed "Is this your card?" .

"You looked again!" He retorted, his face blistered with annoyed expressions. His friends joined with a frown, but I just kept smiling. I clutched the eight of clubs between two of my fingers and flicked it to the side. The crowd snapped their attention to the right, where it should have fallen, but it was nowhere to be seen.

I clapped once.

"Oh no!" I exclaimed again, reaching to the same junifere-brushed ear on the boy. My hand brushed underneath his straw hair, picking the eight of clubs out from behind it. "It isn't nice to steal, you know."

The group of children gasped, whispering to each other feverishly. The boy's blue eyes widened into tidal pools and I was just about ready to crash into them.

"You're a fairy!" He proclaimed, and the children gasped again, mouths agape like a circus had come to town.

"Uh, no, that's—" I started.

The boy crossed his arms. "Then why are your feet bare?"

I looked down at my toes, dusted in dirt from the walk here. Rarely leaving the cottage didn't require needing more than one pair of shoes, and I knew where all the rocks and wasp nests were in the yard, so I usually didn't wear them at all. I had grown so accustomed to the feeling that I had forgotten to put them on now. The children were staring at my feet too, eyes goggling like wild gems. Then they started to giggle. Their laughter strung through the marketplace and wrapped tightly around me.

I laughed along, even as a knot furled in my stomach.

I laughed.

For an instant it was like I was part of the crowd, the group. A pack of friends who knew each other well enough to make those sort of jokes without meaning any real harm.

And for that moment, I allowed myself to pretend it was true.

"Blythe!" Aunt Esther shouted, running up behind me with her satchel bursting with pots of honey. She took me by the shoulders, swiveling me around so my back turned to the crowd. Embarrassment boiled in my cheeks as I stared into her frightened hazel eyes.

"It's fine, it's fine! They just thought I was a fairy!" I whispered, pulling her hands from my shoulders.

She threw her hands back on my shoulders again, grasping tighter. "And what did you tell them?"

"Nothing. They seemed to like me being a fairy…" I glanced back at the crowd, who poorly tried to hide their stares.

"But you're not a fairy, Blythe," Aunt Esther went on, glancing at the toys the children held in their hands. Princesses and knights battling dragons and wicked witches. "You aren't a fairytale that puts children to sleep."

"Gee, thanks, Auntie."

"This is serious, Blythe."

"I know it is!" I ripped her hands from my shoulders, not caring if the raw volume of my voice reached the crowd. The frustrating indecision in picking a branch resurfaced. The monotonous routine of our daily life churned as thick as old cheese. I seethed in frustration for being reprimanded for one fleeting moment of fun.

The yearning for a connection outside of my aunt burst through its seams. I would even settle for the one only found in the past. "But, who knows. Maybe I am half-fairy. Maybe mom was a fairy. It's not like I would know since you never talk about her, or what she liked, or how she spoke, or I don't know... just what her name was!"

The mention of my mother panged inside Aunt Esther. She caught herself before it consumed her. She exhaled, sinking. "Parading around as someone you are not will wither you before you even realize you are wilting."

Guilt plunged into my chest like a rejected pit from a tree.

She was only half of the people unable to speak of mom. At least she was here.

My aunt tried her best mom impression at twenty-something years old, and though it convinced my father enough, it lost its rationale on me the older I got. She should have been out traveling, *living*, instead of wilting away her eccentric personality that only glistened through if I was good. If I didn't find ways to make her life harder.

"Auntie, I'm—"

"It's alright, my love." She placed her palm on my shoulder. After sixteen years of this, she had already nested in the

feeling and made peace with the bruise that never seemed to heal.
"Let's just go home." We strolled out into the beating sun. I
couldn't look back at the boy.

The griffapuff's squawking had whittled down to
whimpers when we returned. I dumped the seemingly never-
ending pots of honey into the brew and *cut, and mixed, and
poured* quicker than ever before. I dashed outside to Aunt Esther
who stayed stroking the griffapuff's head rhythmically as she sang
a calming charm. I handed her the bowl filled with dandelion-
colored paste and crouched beside her.

Aunt Esther had taught me about these creatures years
ago. Griffapuffs live independently from the start of their lives,
fend for themselves, and stake out their food until they mature.
This is achieved when the griffapuff excels in all areas necessary
for survival. It is then they join their flock—or pride. They stay
with those same griffapuffs through and through, carrying out any
task demanded of their pride and going to any length to ensure the
safety of their members. Their family. *Just a little more practice,
friend. Then your people will come for you.*

The griffapuff's moans subsided as my aunt finished off
dressing the wound. The sealant settled, and pink skin started to
close over the wound. After a few minutes, the griffapuff lifted
itself to its feet. I gazed up at the creature who stood at the height

of a very large dog, circling around, testing its strength, its golden talons stretching against the yard. It turned its head to me and its black eyes met mine, twinkling like a river at high noon. Bowing its head, the griffapuff backed away and started galloping, sprinting, then springing above the trees and into the cloudless sky. Flapping its golden wings, it soared beyond our cottage, beyond the marketplace, beyond the limits of gravity.

Aunt Esther let out a relieved sigh, looked at me, and smiled. "Alright, time to start your lessons."

As the griffapuff became nothing more than an amber star in the afternoon sky, I wondered what it would be like for Aunt Esther, for me, if I could soar away too.

That evening, I charted the stars' locations for next season, counted each plant's leaves in our greenhouse to ensure they were growing properly, and learned the various ways to ask a phoenix for one of its feathers. I coaxed myself to bed only at the reminder that tomorrow was Saturday, and I dreamt pleasantly of doing nothing at all the next day.

CHAPTER 3

THE DAY

"I told you I didn't mean to. He saw me in the living room window—from the path some of the townspeople confuse as a way to the river—" I rambled, trying to postpone the inevitable. "And… I don't know… I was excited!"

Aunt Esther exhaled deeply in what I assumed was a fruitless attempt at releasing the tension.

I continued slowly. "I thought it would be funny if I levitated the jewelry hand and waved it at him…" I turned away from my Aunt's searching eyes. "He didn't like it."

Aunt Esther rubbed her temple, trying to regain a calm attitude. "Blythe, that does not give you the right to throw a rock at him."

"He threw the rock at me first! Whole!" I exclaimed, instantly regretting the comment. The glimmer of calm shrunk from my Aunt's eyes as they widened like a tunnel with no foreseeable end.

"YOU WERE ABLE TO BREAK THE ROCK UP?"

I subconsciously scrunched into my shoulders as if I was a turtle. At that moment, I wouldn't mind being a turtle.

Last year, my Aunt demonstrated something similar…ish. Only once. I had been working feverishly to perfect one of the hardest brews in my advanced witchcraft textbook. I could still remember how my muscles ached as I stirred, and grounded, and chopped the ingredients. How my mind felt so tense with pressure that I barely noticed when my elbow knocked a glass jar of dragon's breath off the counter. Aunt Esther heard the swish of the jar hurtling towards my feet and raised her hands as if she could stop it from her place by the stove. To my surprise, and later, gratitude, she did. The jar hovered in mid-air until Aunt Esther scurried over and placed it on the counter, saving my toes from not only being bloodied, but scorched. I instantly snapped out of my bone-aching weariness and gleamed up at my aunt, wide eyes begging to understand how it happened.

"Some witches," she explained. "Are able to wield high magic in times of desperation, or other great feelings."

Little know-it-all Blythe's mind reeled at the notion. "But —but—witches can only practice magic with the help of aids such as herbs, potions, tarot cards, or… or… the elements, " I reminded her.

19

"*This* type of magic can only be utilized in the most extraordinary of circumstances." Aunt Esther caressed my face as if she was checking me for impossible injuries. "Or by the most extraordinary of beings."

As much as I wanted to say I was overcome with anger about the boy's disdain—prejudice—towards me, that that was what allowed me to disassemble the rock and hurl it far enough to scratch him, I couldn't look into the face that only wished to keep me safe and lie. It didn't take a seasoned witch, or a witch at all, to know the power I used was something *other*.

I felt my aunt slump next to me with a mixture of disbelief and sorrow that seeped into my shell. We sat on the stone wall in front of our cottage, silent and still, as the sun finished its bow down to the trees. It was only until our stomachs' growled simultaneously that we met one another's gaze and giggled. I leaned into her, feeling her long, strawberry blonde curls fall over my face like a golden curtain, a reminder that even though she is only my half-aunt, that was enough to tell we are family.

"Are you mad at me?" I let out, still staying sheltered in her curls and flowing navy dress.

"No." She rubbed her hands across my back and held me closer. "No, I am not mad. Yes, you shouldn't have hit him, but…" She leaned away and cupped my face in her hands, where I could see every crease in her olive skin from laughing, crying, and somehow, smiling the most. "I'm not mad you used your magic." She knew that was my fear. She just knew, like aunts did.

I exhaled with relief before realizing what that meant for me. She put her hands in her lap and gazed out into the trees that surrounded our cottage. I looked out too. We let our lawn grow out into a meadow and it teemed with any kind of wildflower that wished to take residence. I would miss greeting the new inhabitants.

I turned to her, trying to restrain myself from sounding too much like a child. "Does this mean I have to go?"

Her gaze dropped to her hands as she tried to maintain her usual content smile, but I could see her knuckles whitening as she clutched her hands.

"I'm not a good enough teacher for…" My heart sank as she searched for a word to describe what I had done. Who I had just changed myself into. *"This,"* she settled on. She shook her head, trying to avoid the unspoken solution. The only reasonable option. "Maybe if dad came back, he would know what to do." I remained silent. Invoking the presence of my father was daunting for us both. "He would know what to do." She reminded me. He was a *man* born with magic, and there was no denying the power in that. While anyone could mix together herbs or give a tarot reading, it took someone with a witchcrafting *gene* to actually infuse said practice with magic. Women were typically the only ones able to *use* the gene, but he demonstrated his power young—

a rare and cherished abnormality in the family. As a grown up, he traveled the world disguised as a doctor, aiding people with his "miraculous" skills—they'd say. "If he can just come back for a little while…"

"Can we wait that long? If my power remains dormant…," I started.

"…It will find a way out." She finished for me, lightening the truth. But, with the high power level I had demonstrated, so young, nonetheless, who knew what could happen to me if my power went untamed. I lowered my head, and Aunt Esther caught my despair before it could consume me. She took my hands in hers, the metal of her rings cool.

"Hey! Now you can make some friends!" She smiled with a false joy in her hazel eyes. She and my father had been concerned about my mingling with others. You never could know how people would react to the unexplainable. Sending me to a school for a bunch of unexplainable persons seemed like an easy way to help these "people" find me. The flicker of fear in their eyes prevented me from probing further.

The same apprehension ignited in me as well now, kindling in the cruelty towards the griffapuff. The reaction of the boy.

"I know this is a big step, but…" She swallowed. "I think your mom would want this for you."

MADISON MCMAHON

Mom. Someone besides me had mentioned my mom.

Acknowledged her existence that seemed excruciatingly far away.

I grabbed onto Aunt Esther and hugged her close. She held me tighter.

"I'll go to Esalroth."

CHAPTER 4

Esalroth Academy of the Mythical, Magical, and Monstrous was built in the fashion you would expect any mythical, magical, and monstrous being would enjoy living in. The greatness of the Gothic mansion loomed over me in a way that caused even more unease than I already felt. It was nothing like our one-story cottage. The windows were not pale green shutters, painted to add life to the humble house, but intricately carved to add to the already illustrious building. Towers and domes protruded from the top of the roof in different sizes, with spikes or small statues poised on top of them. The house itself was burgundy, and the accents an even darker shade, contrasting the lively green of the heavily wooded forest surrounding it. That was all my aunt and I could see through the black metal gate that guarded the front courtyard.

I packed my only possessions in a backpack and a small suitcase, but it felt like I was carrying dead weight in my nervous arms. A flurry of emotions racked my mind. *I'm going to make friends. Friends! What if I don't? What if they don't like me? Goddesses above, why is this house so big? Will I share a room with someone? What type of people will I meet? What if they don't like me? Will my Aunt be ok by herself? Will I?*

My thoughts must have been so abundant that they spilled out of my head and pooled in front of my aunt. She placed her hands on my shoulders. They felt worn in the most comforting ways, like she had crafted every ounce of love in her own hands.

She smiled intensely and said, "You—" The rest of the words caught in her throat and she turned her head away, tightening her grip on me slightly. "Please, behave. Hone your power and do not be afraid of it. You are it and it is you. You have nothing to fear if you trust in yourself. Not your father. You." I was taken aback by her jab at my father, no matter how slight. I had never heard her speak mildly ill of him, even when he would leave abruptly for another trip, giving my young aunt little to no notice.

At that moment, it did not matter. A goodbye that I could hold onto until winter break did. The only one I could conjure was one taught to me by the whispering trees and silent flowers. Admiration. I gazed a second longer at every part that formed Aunt Esther. Her always flowing attire. Her dedication to wearing as many rings as she could pack onto her fingers. The way her nose had a subtle vertical indent in the middle. Her hair. My hair.

She ran her finger across the two tiny braids she weaved on either side of my face, leaving the rest of my hair down.

"I'm going to make you proud," I promised. Aunt Esther went to speak, but the gates creaked open, and I knew someone was there waiting. *Please, I'm not ready yet*, I pleaded with time. I embraced Aunt Esther tight enough to remember she always smelled like the summer air, no matter the season. Aunt Esther let go first, then glanced at the gates.

I didn't dare look.

"I'll be good," I reassured her.

"Good. Be you." She started to walk back to the path we took from our home. Before I left, I shut my bedroom door so she wouldn't have to look at how empty it was.

"Wait!" I called out to her. "What…," I started, finding it harder to ask the question that had been scratching quietly in my mind. At least it would keep her here, if only for another second. "Why do you think mom would want me to go here?"

Aunt Esther gazed at Esalroth wistfully. "I'm sure someone here will help you figure it out."

She continued down the path, not looking back. I watched her until she vanished over the hill.

I commanded myself to take a deep breath. I imagined feeling calm. I could be calm. *I am calm*, I had to tell myself. *Lie until you believe it.*

I turned and saw a hoard of eager faces through the bars of the gate. *Gods below, did they watch all that?* In the front and center of the crowd was an abnormally tall person wearing a long white coat. His pale skin matched his white hair, frayed out from his head, giving the impression he was one of those sage old men that led heroes on their quest in fairy tales. Considering this was Esalroth, the assumption couldn't be too far-fetched.

He kept an appropriate smile as I walked towards the now open gates. All of the other students seemed ready to pounce on me with excitement. *Do they not get a lot of new students?* I wondered.

"Hello, Miss Seraphin. We are so happy you have decided to join us here at Esalroth." His voice was even, but the way his eyes lingered on me indicated some eagerness was itching away at him too. "I am Headmaster Tenold."

"Lift the building off the ground!" A kid with hooves for feet blurted out, clopping excitedly.

"Lift ME off the ground!" A pointy-eared child no older than twelve chimed in. The surrounding group shook their heads vigorously in agreement, eyes wild with intrigue at… me?

"I don't—" I started to reply, but quickly realized what they were referencing. *The accident.*

"Alright, alright, children. Let's allow our new friend to settle in before we demand she commits property destruction." An adult voice emerged from the back. "Or assault." The adult tapped the elfish child on the nose, making her ears wiggle as she chortled. The woman emerged further from the crowd, her dark skin like a deep sea that glistened no matter if the sun shined. A midnight blue cape embroidered with golden stars rippled down her back.

"It's nice to finally meet you, Miss Seraphin. I'm Professor Norwood," she said.

"Yeah, and she teaches the most *boring* subject," The elf child chirped. Still smiling at me, Professor Norwood placed her hand on the child's face and gave her a playful push.

"It's nice to meet you all," I managed to reply. Headmaster Tenold stepped forward, his brown dress shoes clicking on the stone walkway.

"Miss Melsella will show you around briefly and then to your room so you may unpack." He gestured to a girl about my age in front of the crowd. You could only tell she was a teenager from the youth of her face as her hair was long and gray, spinning down her back in loose curls. Her taupe white dress appeared to be blowing in the breeze, despite the lack of wind on that hot summer day. As I looked closer at her, I realized that not only were her feet bare, but they were floating off the ground. She noticed my dumbfounded expression once I saw the little white wings strapped to her ankles and grinned.

I quickly turned back to the Professor.

"Miss Erden and Mr. Thesson can take your bags to your room so you're not lugging them around," Professor Norwood added.

"Oh, I'm fi—" Before I could finish my sentence, the elf and the centaur were removing my bags and prancing into the mansion.

"Right this way." The gray-haired girl smiled, looping her arm in mine—feet now firmly on the ground. The crowd parted for us, still gaping and whispering excitedly. Headmaster Tenold laid a hand that lacked circulation on my shoulder before I continued through.

"Once you have finished unpacking, please join me in my office for a brief overview of the school and your classes. Miss Melsella can show you the way."

I nodded and continued through the crowd. Eyes hung on me as they parted for us, and somehow, I felt both incredibly tiny and excruciatingly large. An ant being scrutinized. A sight being remarked.

An older student with shining blue scales lining their neck clutched their heart as I walked past. Their eyes appeared to be holding back tears. They turned to their friend, and whispered, "It has to be her. I can't believe she has *finally, really* come."

CHAPTER 5

Although I kept my head down as I passed through the crowd, trying to avert the strangely excited—or emotional—eyes, I could not help but be greeted by the high, paneled ceilings of Esalroth. The dark wood forming them melted down into the columns lining the walls. Golden light pin-pricked sections of the foyer from the series of ornate, hanging lamps. Students passed through the intricate display of craftsmanship all around them, paying it no mind, as if they were not standing, *living*, in a painting.

"You must be wondering who or *what* I am," The gray-haired girl declared, breaking my trance. "I'm a distant relative of Aeolus, god of wind and air." A white cloud shrouded the brown of her eyes as she gave her hands a twirl and a gust of wind blew my hair in disarray. Then, after brushing the tangle from my eyes, I saw she was extending her hand to me. "My name is Melsella."

I shook it hesitantly, wondering if she would launch me off my feet as her next trick.

"What's your first name?" I asked, performing the same friendly expressions I had seen the guffawing children in the marketplace make.

"What?" She raised an eyebrow, and I tried to smile at her confusion.

"The Headmaster called you *Miss* Melsella."

Apparently, that was the funniest thing I had ever said because she doubled over with laughter.

She wiped a laughing tear from her eye. "You really are from the *country* countryside."

"Sorry?" I asked. *How in over my head am I?*

"Gods do not have something as silly as last names. What is the need? I am not just any Melsella. I am *the* Melsella. Quite fitting for me, don't you think?" Melsella posed like a statue from the Greek art exhibit. I could not tell if I was amused or annoyed by her just yet, but I figured I'd find out soon.

"My name is—"

"Blythe Seraphin. You like to joke, don't you?" She asked —still smiling—as we ascended the velvet staircase in the center of the foyer.

"Not as much as you like stillness," I jested.

Melsella gave a breathy laugh, clearly feigning understanding of my quip. As we neared the top, three separate hallways sprawled out. The ones to the left and right had similar archways of dark wood, but the one in the center had an arch of marble.

"These are the dormitories. They are separated by species, or, which type of 'M' you are." Melsella snickered. "To the left, you'll find anyone magical. This consists of fairies, elves, centaurs, mermaids, anyone like that." Melsella said that as casually as listing off groceries. The lives these fantastic beings must have lived filled my mind with wonder. *Imagine the adventures they could share. Would they share them with me?*

My stomach levitated, giddy at the idea that I would soon be forging these new experiences. Before Melsella could lead me, I started down the magical hall myself, my boots nearly catching on the purple carpet. *Who would be my roommate? A gnome? A pixie? A—* A brisk hand gripped my wrist and turned me back.

"Where are you going?" Melsella asked with furrowed brows.

"You said this is the magical hall. I'm a witch so…" I let her fill in the blanks I assumed were obvious.

"Oh, no, no, no. *You* will be in the mythical hall," she explained, leading me down the center white marble hallway before I could reply.

"Wait," I said, planting my feet down. "What about that hallway?" I pointed to the right hallway, which seemed strangely darker despite my counting that it had the same amount of lamps lining its walls as the other two hallways.

"Oh," Melsella's demeanor dissipated. She slipped into a whisper. "That's the monstrous hall. Gargoyles, vampires…" She shivered. "Not the best crowd to get involved with. Luckily," She perked up, dragging me down the mythical hall. The contrast of the dark oak floor highlighted the light blue carpet that guided us. Each door matched the impressive white of the marble framing them. Melsella stopped at the one with golden wings painted on it.

"We will be roommates," she beamed, clutching her hands in excitement. "We don't usually share rooms, but we weren't expecting another student so soon. Do not worry. I do *not* snore. And I am sure the Headmaster will set up an opening enchantment for you too. But for now, you will just have to be with me at dinner so I can let us into our room." With that, she lifted her ankle, tapping the white wings strapped to it on the door. It opened slowly as if someone was pulling it with a string on the other side. I had seen magic (I was a witch after all), but to have enchantments to do something as simple as open doors? People who can blow out lamps with the flick of a hand? That was *entirely* new.

THE SON OF MARA

Thin cream and gold stripes reached from floor to ceiling, matching the hues of the lamps sitting on the two desks on opposite sides of the room. On one side sat a neatly made bed with grey sheets and a cloud shaped pillow. To the other, my backpack and suitcase were laid kindly on a bed with crisp white sheets.

"I gave you the window side," Melsella added, pointing to the large window over my bed that would be pretty hard to miss.

"Thank you." I smiled earnestly. She, of all people, must enjoy the breeze.

Unpacking my bags took an embarrassingly brief amount of time. I slipped my tarot deck under my pillow so it would get used to the new energy I would create in Esalroth. Next to my candles, I placed my miniature jars of jasmine, rue, orris root, *honey*, and other mixtures onto my desk. Aunt Esther's words rang through my head, saying, "*A good witch is a prepared witch*". As I pulled out the pencils and notebooks my aunt salvaged from her school days, I had to bat away the crisp reverberation of her voice. It would only make adjusting harder.

I glanced at Melsella who kept herself busy rearranging her own chest of clothes. Ruffles, puffed sleeves, and lace in shades of pure white, storm grey, and the occasional silver burst out as she refolded the wrinkless dresses. My only three dresses and sole nightgown looked like a stain against her and the room's pristine color palette.

Melsella noticed my staring and I quickly resumed unpacking. She glanced over at the clothes I was stuffing into the school-issued chest, only letting her mouth drop an inch before she caught herself.

"You can borrow my clothes any time. They were made to show I come from a family of gods," she gleamed. I couldn't tell if I should be honored or insulted at the gesture.

"Oh, um, thanks," I replied.

"Get used to the special treatment." Her smile widened even higher, teeth glistening like they were carved of white marble.

"So you don't get a lot of new students then?" I asked. Maybe all the fanfare was just students excited by newcomers. Melsella's storm-colored eyebrows raised in surprise. My confusion was no longer funny.

"Who do you think you are?" She stepped forward. *I had done it now. I had learned how to tell a pixie from a sprite by the scent of their home and differentiate a smooth sumac plant from a tree-of-heaven just by touching their leaves. Why did Aunt Esther never give me a class in social etiquette?*

"I'm sorry. Did I say something to—"

"No, no. But, how could you not…" She turned away from me for a moment then walked back to the door. Although I had only just met Melsella, I could tell it was a rare occasion for her to be speechless. "I'll take you to Headmaster Tenold."

CHAPTER 6

I had to maintain a light jog to keep in pace with Melsella as we went back down the stairs and to another wing of Esalroth. I could not admire it as well in Melsella's haste, but it appeared to be the school wing, filled with a variety of different classrooms—all unoccupied since it was a Sunday. Every few doors, narrow stairways sprouted upwards and down to unknown destinations.

We turned down several sets of hallways before we came to one with a surprising dead end marked by a wooden door that stood out amongst the rest of the elaborate architecture for how simple it was. A door I might have had at home, the only difference being a thin nameplate engraved in silver, reading: *Headmaster Christer Tenold.*

Melsella turned the knob, which was starting to corrode in a teal shade. A longer, rather than broad, stone corridor was sheathed in a series of tapestries, the most notable among them of a group of people slaying a dragon. I recognized it to be the

Völsunga saga from Norse mythology. As I admired the tapestry closer, the lingering smell of an herb drifted to my nose.

I gave the back of Melsella's head a quick glance before I peered behind the tapestry. I congratulated myself and silently thanked Aunt Esther for her rigorous schooling. My suspicions were correct. Behind the tapestry was a glass case screwed onto the wall, containing a simple wooden staff with ginger root wrapped around the base of the staff, infusing it with its power-based capabilities.

The Headmaster must be a practitioner, but from the dust collecting on the case, apparently a dormant one. However, unlike witches, this was no problem at all as the power he possessed was only able to be accessed with his staff in hand.

"Come." Melsella nodded for me to keep up as I jolted away from the tapestry. I continued alongside her to the end of the corridor, each step making me wish I had worn a sweater to fend off the coolness in the air. Headmaster Tenold sat at a plain cedar desk, reading intently over a scatter of papers, no photograph or personal belonging there to find solace in. "I have brought Blythe, Headmaster."

He looked up at me, something unreadable in his eyes. "Thank you, Miss Melsella. You may leave us." Melsella nodded and smiled at me before kicking off the ground and floating back the way we came. A gust of wind rushed from her, increasing the chill.

Headmaster Tenold stood up, eyes fixed on me, and walked to the front of his desk, his dress shoes clacking even more sharply than before. The dim lighting of his office stressed the premature wrinkles under his eyes and streaking his forehead. Even though the Headmaster's white hair thinned like any old man's would, the trying composure he held himself in revealed those were not the marks of time, but stress. Beneath laid a weathered man slightly older than my aunt.

He crossed his arms over his long white coat. "I trust you are liking everything at Esalroth so far," he declared. I almost grimaced at his confidence, but it would be foolish of anyone to deny the place was not absolutely enchanting. As I looked at his two bookcases, too small to fit his moderate collection of books, I realized he must have had to give up his own comfort to allow it to remain so decadent.

"Yes, it really is all wonderful. But—" The use of the conjunction made him stand up straighter, fearing I may not like something. "I asked Melsella and she gave me a pretty strange answer, but do you not get a lot of students here? The way people look at me it's…"

THE SON OF MARA

"Something you will have to get used to," he finished for me, a grin quirking in his ashen lips. "We have been waiting for you for," He looked to the tapestries. "A long time."

"I don't follow." I shook my head, eyes searching desperately for the clue to make me understand what everyone saw when they gaped at me. What everyone meant when they spoke to me.

"You see…." The Headmaster started to speak, but became tangled in his words. Then, face growing alight, struck with an idea, he turned to his bookshelf and wrangled a red cover out from its tightly tucked spot. He opened it and pulled out a single piece of paper. "I suggest reading may help you understand better." He held out the paper to me as he sat down. I took it, its ink sunken in with age against the delicate page.

The Son of Mara shall return to fulfill his mother's wrath.
The one to save all must be led down the right path.
As one grows stronger, so shall the other.
But the power of the chosen one will make all stutter.

I wrinkled my brow. What is this?

"Is this a riddle I have to pass to be accepted? Or…" I let my words fade, for once hoping somebody else would finish them.

"No, Miss Seraphin. This is you," he elucidated, pointing to the page clutched in my growingly sweaty hands. Cold sweats.

"I don't... I don't follow," I repeated. Who is the Son of Mara? What even is Mara?

A smile fledged across his face. "Well, I don't know about your aunt, but I definitely stuttered when I heard of a witch using magic unaided, so young, nonetheless."

What.

The Headmaster picked up on my bewilderment and stood, moving to the front of his desk, closer to me this time. He brushed by a few papers teetering on the edge of his desk, allowing them to sway to the floor in his... *urgency?*

"Out of the handful of schools for magical youth, Esalroth has all the best professors and curriculum to assist you," The Headmaster assured me, his faint brows rising and falling in an effort to be more convincing.

"Assist me?" I repeated once more. I was no fool. I read the page over again in my mind, increasing the pace, searching for a hidden phrase tucked between a letter or two that would wash away all the confusion as quickly as a pesky bug found in the sink.

"We have many talented students who would be more than happy to help you in your studies should your training take up most of your time."

It was then I could read his eyes. They were longing.

"Training?" I attempted to swallow past the lump in my throat, but that did nothing for my spinning head and clammy palms. "Headmaster, have I read into…" I scanned the paper again, unsure of what to call it.

"There is only one way to read the prophecy," he asserted, lacing his fingers over one another.

"The… the *prophecy*? Sir, you…" I fumbled over my words, scouring for any other explanation than the most evident. The most likely. The most daunting.

The intensity of his pale blue eyes yanked me from unspooling the rest of my loose thoughts. The patience inside the Headmaster finally folded.

"I am a busy person, Blythe, as I am sure you will soon be as well. So let us not walk around this as time may very soon be of the essence."

"Of the what? That is not fair." The Headmaster retracted his head back in surprise at my intolerance. He could go on about how impressive my skills are for my age but not treat me as the mature person he assumes I am? "What you're saying… what I think you're saying… "

The Headmaster's posture grew taut as I drudged on, utterly bewildered. *How long has he been waiting?*

"Say it, child," he urged, the eagerness lurking in his eyes.

Child.

"I'm *the one*," I replied through pinched lips, wishing with every fiber of my being I was wrong. I was ridiculous. Ludicrous, even. With clenched fists and cold, nervous heat permeating from my brow, I looked up at him.

He smiled, leaning back. "You are as smart as your aunt insists."

The compliment should have—would have—made me beam with pride, but instead, it left me trembling.

He gave a simple nod as if he could not, or didn't care to, see my troubled expression. "Welcome to Esalroth."

With that, I ran down the corridor and out the door.

CHAPTER 7

The labyrinth of Esalroth contorted itself further in my distress. Every turn was another hallway of dark oak and towering arches. I dashed down anywhere, *praying* that every step was increasing the space between the Headmaster and myself. I pounded any worries out of my head with the hurried, desperate steps of my feet.

Murmurs slithered from the upcoming hall to the right.

Damnit.

I spun left.

A double-arched door left slightly ajar stopped me, almost causing me to trip over the laces of my boots. I looked down at them. The mud outside the cottage shed was caked onto the toes. Aunt Esther would have insisted I return the dirt home before its family missed it too dearly. The thought of her left my stomach in a knot.

I slipped through the door and shut it with the weight of my body, sliding down into a crouch, fastening my eyes tight. The cold of the frigid tile floor immediately penetrated through the thin layer of my tan dress. Worries, fears, anxieties, snaked around my head, pressurizing it until all I could feel was the bloated weight of my brain. I had a sole, simple task to do—learn to control my power, make a pal or two, and return back to my proud aunt. *That?* That was something I could not comprehend, which only made the snake coil tighter.

I gave into the weight of my head and let it collapse in my hands, circulation fizzling from my frantic escape, coupled with the chill of every damned place in that castle.

Then, I laughed. I laughed at the absurdity of it all. The illogical, nonsensical lie that these people believed in so terribly their eyes plucked with tears at the sight of me—the face that salvaged the remaining hope all would be saved from the force of an unimaginable beast.

"We have couches, you know," a low voice announced. I jerked back, whacking my head on the heavy wooden door. Hair that waved like a velvet midnight looked down at me, his dark eyes observing me quizzically. "No need to beat yourself up over it," he said earnestly. "They're ancient with time but softer than the floor."

It was then the vastness of the room came into view like a curtain unveiling the stage of a play. Mahogany shelves scaled their way to the arched ceiling that I dared to think was the height of Esalroth itself, making the number of books not equal to one but four stories. Warm-toned furniture posed under the gaze of regal self-portraits, vivid landscapes, and captivating scenes—all encased in golden frames. Candelabras stood on polished desks, accompanied by the furniture pushed up towards them for more comfortable studying.

"It's a shame a school has so few books," I commented, unable to avert my eyes from the fantasy encircling me.

"Yeah, I'm sure they would shut us down if the majority of the students could not brutally maim the council," he added, walking towards a large yellow armchair, hooking his leg over the edge. Then, deciding against it, he settled his feet on the ground, crossing one ankle over the other, allowing himself to be absorbed by the plush cushion back.

"I suppose I'll have to settle." I plopped down on a red sofa across from him. The harsh yellow of the armchair highlighted the strokes of midnight blue in his dark hair. A black tunic puffed out from under his fitted ink vest, giving the impression he was hatched from the tall shadows of the bookcases.

"So," He fiddled with his nails. "Have you had the talk yet?"

My eyebrows pinched together. "Excuse me?"

A flush of red surfaced through his light brown skin. "No, no, that's not what I meant." He exhaled a breathy, nervous laugh. "What I meant was," He bit his bottom lip, eyes searching the ground before deciding on his approach. "I'm Dante."

"Blythe...," I returned hesitantly.

"Yes, I know." Dante offered a tight lipped smile, stumbling to alleviate the confusion. "I meant the talk with Tenold. You're—"

"No." The word shot from my tongue with a harsh finality as a dense heat germinated in my spine and crept across my brow. *The library must have had a hidden fireplace brewing in its furniture. That wouldn't be all that surprising, now.*

"What?" Dante cocked an eyebrow, straightening out of his lazing stance.

"I'm only a witch," I reminded myself more than him.

"Actually, you're 'only' all everyone has been hoping for." He brushed fake dust off his sleeve, the bones of his hands as strikingly defined as the keys of a piano.

"I'm only here to perfect my power and go home, thank you." The sentence left my lips sounding more like a plea. Dread clutched at my throat, and I felt every fiber of fabric gnawing at my skin.

"Not before you defeat the son of a demon, unfortunately." He grinned into the knuckle of his hand, covering a part in his lips.

"This isn't like… a metaphorical demon?" I asked, wishing hopelessly.

Dante rose from his seat with a swift turn, giving a hearty chuckle as he wandered off. His lanky figure disappeared behind a tall lamp. I followed the walking shadow, preferring his presence to the one undoubtedly searching for me. He grazed his fingers along the spines of books, tracing their lettering until he came to a sizable battered book. *Curses, Demons, and Other Shockingly Revolting and Horrifying Beings* glided from its spot with ease as if it had been pulled out numerous times. Upon first glance, the tattered edges and aged pages gave the illusion it was well-loved. As Dante opened the book, the facade was swallowed up by the sinister yawn it gave. As if it had been waiting.

"Unlikely with a mother like that." Dante turned the book to me, pointing to a collage composed of different women who possessed an undead skeletal figure, jagged teeth, or a combination of the most grotesque insects' features.

"Which one is Mara?" I asked, taking the book from him, accidentally brushing against his hands that made the frigid tile floor feel like a summer breeze. He pulled back, looking down while tracing the knuckle of his index finger methodically.

"We're not really sure. She's been around for centuries with different variations in each culture and religion. One says she is the devil's older sister. One claims she's the physical personification of evil. Another," He took the book, turning the page gingerly as he stared into the words etched into the paper. "Believes she is the reason children have nightmares."

"Why is Mara—er, rather,—her son, returning to finish her wrath? What was she so vengeful about?" The question felt like a line in a play, or a quest for a knight. The entire day exuded the uneasy haze of a dream so bizarre your first instinct was to call it a nightmare.

"Similarly, it's also debated. The only certainty is that Mara was exorcised 16 odd years ago, leaving a son in her wake. And when the one returns, so does the son." He snapped the book shut, containing its thickening presence. "One theory is that her son is returning to punish the world for vanquishing his mother. Another theory is he is here for the same reason Mara was, but with the one thing she lacked that may have kept her killing for centuries longer. A reason."

My shoulders drooped as the gravity sank in. "Who…" I could feel my thoughts clogging my throat, each one clambering to be voiced. "Who is the son?"

Dante caught hold of my grim expression, sobering his own in sympathy. "Another mystery."

"No, this is… it's impossible." I shook my head, pacing the carpeted floor. "That 'prophecy' was as vague as can be about 'the one'. Anyone stutters at powers they do not yet understand."

Dante kept in his place, eyes keeping in step with my pace. "But all stutter at a witch who has the focus to disassemble the makeup of a rock and the will power to launch it so far—even if they understand witchcraft."

The library pivoted and my brain insisted the towering shelves were caving in from the damp heat teeming from my every pore. I felt each book slick with sweat and each chair, lounge, and ottoman sodden with unforgiving moisture. The inferno crawled closer until it bogged my ears with an August swamp.

This was not what I wanted. This was too much. I thought I was ready for the world, but I was wrong. The idea latched onto my ankles and yanked me down, down, down. My father had been right.

Was my father right?

Get out, get out, get out, get out, a voice squeaked in the last untouched crevice of my mind. I stumbled back, tripping on the divot in the carpet. My hands thrust myself up from the parched rug, grasping for the door that felt like it was only stretching farther away.

"Don't!" Dante cried, his voice peaking in illegible desperation. I halted, twisting my head to the shelf we just stood at. Only then, he suddenly stood inches from me while I panted for air. He faltered as he unraveled his hand from the other, stretching it out towards me, eyes whispering to mine if that was all right. And, it was.

He laid his hand on my bare bicep and a fresh pool of rain blossomed inside of me. The kind that comes to relieve the grass of its compacted heat and is welcomed to nestle in the blades. Then, he placed his other hand on my neck and a blanket of snowfall curled around me like a scarf. I blinked up at him, a breeze returning to my lungs. For a moment, just one, the gazes of our eyes tunneled to one another, cloaked in a summer's midnight, cold, and warm, and inviting.

Dante withdrew his hands to the pockets of his black pants, the creases of it accentuated by the dull light emanating from the sconces at the door.

"I have read to the woman who burns books," said Dante, gesturing to the painting in the dead center of the library that pictured a woman shrouded in stacks of books starting to burn from the candles melting atop them.

"Oh, that's… nice of you." *I've never heard of a creature who takes shape in a painting before*, I thought.

"No, I've read all the books on the shelves up to *that* painting."

Oh.

Oh indeed. Volumes upon volumes of books resided in those shelves, floor to ceiling, novella to encyclopedia. *How long has he been here?*

Dante stared down, tracing the bed of his thumb with his nail. "I'm sure if we both read the rest we could learn more about Mara and her history, and then determine who and where her son is and could be." He looked up at me, eyes shy in wonder.

"Then I'll know what I'm up against." My relief rose into a smile. *I'll train effectively and just… save the world… whenever that may be. Not easy, but easier enough.* I looked at Dante. "It's astounding how you make do with so little enrichment."

Eyes still retreated from me, he spit out a laugh. His teeth gleamed dramatically, contrasting the deep shadow of his apparel. As Dante's grin widened, a fang poked out of the corner, and before he could even glimpse at my reaction, he felt my rush of realization.

He snapped his mouth shut, spinning his head from me, feet unable to free themselves from the stonery of feeling caught.

I stepped towards him. "My aunt read me stories about you." His posture clenched, bracing. "I thought you would have worn a cape."

He turned back, relief wavering in the grin he let extend freely, then with words that flowed like a stream, he said, "It's nice to meet you, Blythe Seraphin."

"It's nice to meet you, Dante…"

"Shyung," he answered.

I extended my hand to him. For a moment, he looked at it as if it was the first to be offered to him. He took it.

"The pleasure is all mine, Dante Shyung."

CHAPTER 8

The first echo of a bell made my mind stumble, thinking Aunt Esther was calling me to jam spread generously on toast and tea with a heavy emphasis on the sugar. But as the bell rang deeper, it was clear the sound could not be the tinny ring from our little chime.

Dante explained that the low hum came from the Bell, which rang three times for meals and once at the start and end of class periods. Unfortunately, no one knew where the Bell was located, so it could not be bewitched to have lunch come just five minutes earlier. We played a weird game of start and stop while he guided me towards the dining hall in an ambling stroll. I skittered as far ahead as I could while maintaining a sense of direction, keeping an eye out for a flustered Headmaster. Dante eyed me strangely, but clearly thought better not to ask.

After a series of turns and twists that it would take me months to familiarize myself with, we came to a double-arched doorway, like one of a boastful chapel or a welcoming dungeon.

The doors were propped open to reveal the most breathtaking

room in Esalroth. The ceiling—as that was always the first piece

of architecture that hailed notice at Esalroth—had similar

coffering to the library, but instead of wood, smooth ivory stone

accented the panels and lunged down the columns supporting the

structure. On the back wall, one massive, golden, Palladian

window heralded beams of sunlight to sequences of round tables

clothed in crimson, the light gliding across the circles of satin, like

a moonlit river. Above it all floated a grand chandelier beaded in

clear crystals. It was a ballroom turned cafeteria.

As Dante and I passed through the room, clinging to the

walls that offered some relative shade, students chattered and

smacked on a variety of cuisines. However, I did not see a place

to grab a meal, or a kitchen large enough to provide such options.

"Danny!" a high voice exclaimed. A blur of black,

yellow, and white rushed towards us. The person, a year or two

older than Dante and myself, had skin not European white, but

eggshell white—the kind you painted the accents of your shed.

Black antennas poked out from her forehead, which gave way to

her long raven hair.

"Is this she?" the person asked excitedly, pointing two

of her four arms at me. Dante smirked at her in confirmation. Her

yellow eyes widened with a squeal and hurtled into me, absorbing

me in the most feeling hug.

"I'm Clyde. Well, Clymene. Like the moth, duh," she explained, gesturing to her wings that rested behind the knee-length ruffles of her short gothic dress. I gawked in amazement. Black antennas, yellow eyes, and triangular white wings...

"You're a haploa clymene moth! We almost never saw you in our yard. Do you really have a..." My voice trailed off, uncertain if the question was appropriate. Thankfully, Clyde's face went alight with knowing as she rotated, revealing her wings. Lines of charcoal outlined the alabaster appendages. A single black streak bled down the center and splintered into two short lines, forming an upside down cross.

"Wicked," I mused. Then, remembering, I laughed to myself. "When I was eight, I left strawberries out in hopes of seeing you."

Clyde snorted, putting all four hands on her belly as she chuckled. Dante looked at me with that same humorous knowing look.

"Clyde is—to put it lightly—an avid fan of peaches." Dante gestured to her plate at the table, stacked with fresh peaches, a miniature peach pie, and an orange cup of what I assumed to be peach juice.

"Better than one of blood," responded a voice from under the table. The beak of a white plague doctor mask breached from under the tablecloth, and a short figure plopped down in the cushioned dining chair.

Clyde's black lips frowned as she placed all four hands on her hips, antennas scrunching down with her eyebrows. "Gus, how could you hide from our new friend?"

"I have others." Gus dismissed me. Curiously, his words were crisp despite the heavy mask encasing his face. His only distinguishable features were the pumpernickel hair brushing out from under his wide-brimmed leather hat and his tiny hands, the color of the acorns that peppered the cottage yard in the fall.

"Yeah, yeah, you can talk to Satan's cat or whatever. But now..." Clyde placed two left hands on my shoulder as two right hands ushered me into the dining chair next to her's. "We are in the presence of the one, Gustavo!" She beamed, clasping her hands together as Gus folded his arms over his all-black suit.

"Wow, my full name. You are serious," mocked Gus. The instantaneous recognition I received threw me off kilter every time, inching heat up my cheeks.

"Where do we get lunch?" I asked, steering the subject.

"Feeding Chuck, of course," Clyde replied. At this point, I didn't even bother uttering a confused what? Who? How? "Blythe, meet Chuck!" Clyde gestured to the golden candelabra with a single holder in front of my place setting. Identical ones—Chucks—stood in front of each of the five place settings at the table, their golden stems basking in the pearl of afternoon light.

To the right of each fork was a simple match kit, containing a singular stick.

"Their name is Chauncey," Gus retorted.

"That's much too pretentious. It doesn't fit *Chuck*." Clyde turned to me with a bright smile that matched the excited yellow of her eyes. "All you do is light the candle and Chuck will bring you what they think you need. You feed them." Clyde extended out the two hands on her right like a mock scale. "They feed you," she said, evening the scale with her left pair of arms.

I took the thin match in my hand and swiped it against the striker. The candlestick—*Chuck*—seemed to straighten in anticipation. The flame immediately took to the wick, and the candle rotated downward, vanishing into the cloth. I flung the drapery up and scoured the underside of the table.

Nothing but Dante's leather shoes, Clyde's slick black doll heels, and Gus' dangling feet lived below.

"Taffies?" Clyde said from above. I pulled my head up and on a fine china plate was a glass bowl of taffies. My eyes widened at the sight. I could identify all of them through its cloudy paper. Caramel resembled a deer with its taupe color and white swirl. Watermelon had a lime green circling the red center. And—how could I not have spotted it first?—*apple pie* appeared the same way an actual pie would, but bite-size and much, much more enticing. Children nibbled on them feverishly in the marketplace, and I had begged Aunt Esther for a pack, even just one. She smiled her well-meaning smile and claimed her apple pie would sour in my mouth for the insulting remark.

I shed the wrapper from the candy and shoveled it into my mouth. The scent of heated cobblestone, newly imported linens, and wooden booths swelled my senses as the gooiness melted happily on my tongue. Upon my third (or was it fifth?) piece, my tongue pleaded for hydration. I looked to my right, and a crystal glass of iced tea winked back at me, a heap of sugar clumping at the bottom.

Dante and Gus nourished their Chucks, and two plates rose from the satin. Steam twirled from Dante's creamy bowl of soup like phantom acrobats. Flaps of deli meats fanned out around Gus' plate, which, every so often, he would lower under the table, a piece or two disappearing each time it resurfaced. I thought better not to look.

Dante lifted an ornate spoon to his mouth, raising a watchful hand to shield the view of what lay under his lips. If Dante was comfortable with Clyde, Gus, and me, the act was for the table's surrounding us. While I was sure most people knew what Dante was, I guessed he didn't want them to *see* it.

He took a wary sip or two before I could no longer take it. I opened my mouth dramatically wide and made a display of plucking out the bits of taffy thoroughly suctioned to my teeth. Dante's mouth pressed into a smirk while Clyde eyed me as though the sugar had surged through my brain. Then, understanding, she plunged her face into her peach pie. She pulled her head up, and orange goop clung to her nose, cheeks, and chin as she smiled wide, scrunching her eyes closed to keep her irises from tasting her meal. I could hardly keep my bark of a laugh contained. Though I couldn't see them, I could feel Gus roll his eyes and pierce a flap of meat on the pointy nose of his mask. Dante lowered his other hand and took an exposed slurp of his soup.

All of a sudden, Gus scoffed. Dante lifted his knuckle to his lips, pretending as if he were just suppressing a cough, but the flush in his cheeks told otherwise. Clyde gave him a swift kick under the table.

"They're *staring*." Gus nodded to the other tables, and indeed, he was right. Heads alternated between stealing looks as if they had coordinated who would get a peak when.

"They're not staring at us," Dante corrected. He looked at me, his eyes reading mine on whether to be sympathetic or honored. I surveyed the room, taking note of the person with blue scales, eyes noticeably swelling, and the elf, waving feverishly at me as the hoof-footed child yanked the elf's hand down. Then, Melsella, who was trying to disguise the alarming pace she was approaching our table with a startling smile.

"Blytheee," she held onto the last syllable as her voice pinched higher. "I thought you were going to sit with me," she asked rhetorically, intentionally ignoring the rest of the table.

"I thought I only needed to do that for dinner, so I could get back into our room," I answered. Aggravation itched at Melsella's posture.

"Well, I *am* your guide, so I figured you would want," She flicked her eyes to Dante. "Knowledgeable company."

"Good thing we just came from the library," I replied, only giving her the half side of my face. Melsella went to speak, but her words were caught by a hand on her shoulder.

"Miss Melsella," Professor Norwood said. "You wouldn't mind if I borrowed Miss Seraphin, would you?"

I'd been found.

She looked at the table, noticing my other company. "Mr. Shyung? Miss Chaumont? Mr. Jiménez?" They all shook their heads, except Gus, who gave a showy huff.

"Wonderful. Will you join me, Miss Seraphin?" The raise in her smiling cheeks rebounded the warm glow of the sunlight and the fading and flickering Chucks.

"I can save your candies in a baggy," Clyde reassured me, patting her hand on mine, understanding the importance of favorite foods.

"I'll bring it to you tomorrow," added Dante, tracing his fingers on the carvings of the back of the chair. *Tomorrow.* The reminder this wasn't just some hazy dream filled with towering castles and tasked candles.

I nodded. "I'll meet you in the library."

Then, Professor Norwood whisked me away, and it took everything inside me not to voice the plaguing thoughts in my head.

Please do not take me back to the Headmaster.

CHAPTER 9

Professor Norwood led me back to the school wing of
Esalroth and into a classroom covered with the faces of maps
from places I didn't recognize. On one, a dashed line ran across a
plot of land from a red mushroom, to a purple, and then to a
yellow. They must not have simply been mushrooms for they had
doors and windows and were named. Another map was composed
of concentric circles similar to the rings of a planet. I moved
closer, noticing the locations seemed to be orbiting on their own.
A chill ran through me because I was simultaneously unnerved
and excited by the prospect of having something unknown, and
new. A lesson my aunt had yet to teach me.

Professor Norwood unclasped her cerulean cloak and
draped it on the back of her desk chair that appeared as if it could
have been stolen from a kingdom's throne room.

She noticed me staring. "A present from the Headmaster,"
she explained, sitting down. "A worthy enough gift considering

I've been here for almost thirty years." She gave a light laugh, gesturing for me to sit on the lush cushion stool in front of her desk.

"*Thirty* years? But, you don't even look thirty." I replied without thinking, instantly clasping a hand over my mouth. The Professor only chuckled again.

"I haven't taught all those years, no. I became a student here at ten years old. I met your aunt a few years later."

I blinked rapidly. '*I'm sure someone here will help you figure it out*' Aunt Esther had said. "My aunt went here." After all her and my father's clambering for me *not* to go to Esalroth? And what did that have to do with my mother? Did she attend the academy as well? My heart prickled, but I couldn't tell if it was with anger or sadness.

"Esther was a much better student than me in alchemy, creaturology, mystical botany…" She counted the subjects on each finger. "Even history, too. It's funny considering that's what I teach now." There was an ease in her voice that made me feel this was not a conversation between student and teacher, but family friends.

"Are you a witch too?" I asked, leaning closer.

"A psychic sorcerer," she corrected. "I am not as inclined to physically practice magic as say, your aunt, but I can understand magic in ways others seem to struggle with."

I raised a brow. "I thought you said Aunt Esther was a better student than you?"

"The best of students do not merely get good grades. The best students utilize the knowledge." The Professor adjusted a picture frame I could not see the contents of. "Tell me about the boy."

"Who?"

"The one who threw the rock at you." Her calm posture remained as I shifted on the stool, fear shooting up my spine as I caught myself from inching a little too far off the side.

The memories of the accident spewed into my mind like fresh chunks of vomit. The shining blonde locks of the boy that dazzled me. The glee that tickled at me when I thought his giggle at a floating jewelry hand might be as radiant as his hair. Then, the plummet in my chest when he picked up the rock.

"He had a very aggressive way of saying he did not want to be friends," was all I cared to reply.

"Throwing rocks is a very unkind thing to do, yes." She nodded, contemplating. The placid demeanor she bore was a refreshing take from my aunt's and the Headmaster's. I probably would have kept the same attitude would it have not been for a formidable prophecy. "Tell me about how he felt."

"What?" I sputtered back. "Excuse me, it's just... he attacked *me*. Wouldn't it make more sense to ask how I felt?"

65

"Oh, by no means am I trying to diminish that experience for you. I am only trying to understand everything," she replied.

"At first... at first I thought he was angry because of all the vibrating," I explained plainly. "But, when I caught the rock from him, the vibration gave way to the trembling. Which... I don't know. I think it had been there all along."

"What had?" She asked, her brown eyes warm with reassurance.

"Fear. It was fear." I shrunk into my shoulders, uneasy with how honest I could be with a perfect stranger. A person who was not my aunt.

"Hmm," she answered as though I had just given an interesting insight to a homework question. "Tell me about the rock."

"I don't know. It was heavy enough to hurt him," I shrugged like I was back on the stone wall of the cottage, anxious for dinner.

The Professor gave a light snicker before continuing. "How about the space you crossed to feel its weight?"

The recollections of the accident barreled in from the jammed door they were forced behind. The moment I decided no.

"It was like my conscience—or—I don't know..." I shook my head, attempting to disband the embarrassment curdling inside me.

Professor Norwood straightened. "Let yourself continue."

I clenched my fists, summoning the strength to admit what felt so true, so right. "My spirit. It grabbed the rock," I conceded.

"Your spirit?" Professor Norwood repeated.

"Yes," I sat straighter, emboldened by the sheer feeling of speaking *it* aloud. "Like the one that swirls in your chest when you're joyful and stomps in your lungs when it disapproves."

There was a crack in Professor Norwood's posture. She ingested my words like tea you did not assume to be so scorching, but refused to reveal how your tongue burned. Effortlessly, she mended her composure by pacing to the map positioned behind her desk, her black braid swaying in her stride.

"I don't think I need to explain to you that not everyone can physically sense other people's feelings. Nor can most *use* *that* to personify—what you call your spirit—in the way you can," she said as she looked at the aged map, its frayed edges, distorted colors, and wrinkles making it clear it was the oldest one in the room. "You already know that, though. I think you already know a lot of things that might be too frightening to let yourself *understand*." The part of me I kept concealed, *obedient*, squeamed under the scrutiny. She was right. I knew it from the varied reactions between my aunt and me that were beyond a casual difference in care. I knew it in the feelings of others passing by me in the marketplace. I realized I shouldn't have known, or have sensed. I knew I was... different... well before it became externally apparent.

"I was just—" I faltered, retracting from my courage, knowing what accepting it would mean. "I was just angry. Witches can wield high magic when they experience great feelings," I nodded along, mimicking my aunt's words that day in the kitchen.

The Professor turned to me, eyes alight with knowing. "Correct, but then how did you lift the jewelry hand?"

Realization submerged my brain meters underneath the waves of an ice cold ocean. Oceans had separate names, but they were all connected in one limitless sea that all spiraled farther down than one would ever *wish* to imagine. Staring up at the world I knew before, the surface became no more than a dimly lit haze.

The jewelry hand. Then I wasn't angry or scared or anything for that matter. I barely even thought about lifting it. I just... did it.

"Professor," I looked up at her, feeling the weight of confusion sink in my brows and the desire to understand fester in my grey eyes. "What am I?" The vulnerability of the question swelled in the room—the weight of having to ask such a thing, suffocating.

Professor Norwood crossed over to the stool, dissipating the heavy cloud with her easy strides. A thickness in her eyes reminded me of the books packed on the library's shelves. "Do you want to find out?"

CHAPTER 10

"Classroom -66" read the schedule Professor Norwood had given me. My first class—occultism with Professor Sylmaris —would be in Classroom -66. The doors I passed proclaimed they were classroom 40, 1,234, or even 0, but nothing in the negative.

As I searched, stares lit the hallways more than the gilded lamps above them. No matter which way I turned, or no matter how close I drifted to the wall, I was a five and a half foot beacon for prying eyes and fervent whispers.

"Hello," I nodded to a cluster of whispering students, pretending I knew exactly where I was going. They gaped at me, huddling closer together with such glee you would have thought Athena had just admitted to them they were the better weavers.

I turned and pivoted down five more hallways, feigning that I was completely okay with each stare and comment— soaking it in, in fact. This was what I wanted, after all. OR at least… something like that. This was what I wished for on every star that first caught my eye each night since my aunt first told me stars offered those gifts. *This* beat that terrible betrayal of waking up the following day to find the star had faded, along with my unanswered wish.

Upon turning down the sixth hallway—where I could have sworn someone tried to sniff my hair—I accepted that I would be truly late if I did not ask for help. Then, I spotted a boy hunched beneath the lamplight reading a textbook, committing the miraculous act I had seen all morning. He was not staring at me.

As I approached him, a wave of light glided through his tuft of red hair like a strong breeze blowing across a wheat field in the morning. His sage colored skin contrasted the loose blue jacket fitting him.

"Excuse me," I started. The boy jolted back, clenching his textbook with ready yellow claws.

The eyes I had greeted at Esalroth ranged from emotional browns to dazzled blues to green eyes that twinkled like they had just encountered the divine. The pair of burnt orange eyes before me was the first that appeared frightened.

"I didn't mean to startle you, sorry. I'm Blythe. I'm new here." I said, gesturing to the wrinkled schedule in my hands. He continued to stare, but not in the way those littering the halls did. Their eyes reached out with wanting while his retracted in escape. To think I had gone from being mocked in the marketplace to being practically venerated by students to being feared for a greeting was quite a whirlwind to endure in just two days.

"What's your name?" I asked, trying to alleviate what I could only hope was not repulsion. Fame wasn't a very forgivable crime to some.

He pulled himself up a little straighter at the question, easing the grip on his textbook. "Charlie," he answered, the two fangs jutting from his bottom lip wiggled into a smile.

"Lovely to meet you, Charlie! Would you mind pointing me to where classroom negative sixty six is?" The question left me tongue like stiff dialogue from a school play. Unbelievably unreal.

"Just down there, actually," Charlie pointed to a narrow stairway to the left that spiraled down in heavy stone. "I-I'm headed there myself," he added sheepishly.

Relief flowered in my chest. "Thank the goddesses above. I don't know many people yet."

Charlie smiled bashfully, eyes retreating to his tattered black shoes. He took a step towards the stairway entrance, gesturing to it with an unsure hand. "L-ladies first. If you want to, of course," he amended.

"Just this once, I suppose," I smiled back, giving a curtsy before descending down the steps. Portraits of well-dressed teachers lined the rough grey stone walls. A cedar framed portrait depicted a professor dressed in a crimson robe and brown cap next to a globe that spun upside down. The room where he sat was truly medieval, complete with a finely carved desk shrouded in a weaved tapestry. The next portrait consisted of a man in a powdered wig sporting a finely tailored waistcoat with tiny ferns quite literally sprouting out of its hems. These must be previous occultism teachers.

"Oh no," I whipped around to Charlie, who flinched at my sudden movement. I checked my abrupt tone, taking into account suddenance might just be something that overwhelms him. "Professor Norwood never gave me any textbooks."

"Professor Norwood won't give you a textbook until she dies," he answered casually.

"Wh-, excuse me. What?"

"The most recently deceased teacher of the subject hands out the textbooks. See," Charlie pointed to the final painting that hung next to the heavy wooden door with -66 etched in silver onto it. Inside the portrait, a woman with a puffed sleeve Edwardian blouse looked out from her bathtub upon the sea it floated in.

"P-pardon me, Professor Thrall," Charlie tapped on the golden frame and motion bounded through the painting like it was only a tank that needed a gentle knocking to wake the fish.

"Aye, Charlie! Have you seen any crawdads about the water today?" The Professor called to him from her bathtub boat.

"No, Professor. None today," he replied.

"Good. Nasty little buggers they are," Professor Thrall grumbled as she turned her gaze to me, studying my appearance. "Is it a new school year already?"

"No, Professor. She is just new."

"Aye, so you will be needing a book then, love?" The Professor asked. I managed to nod, trying to keep from looking too bewildered that a painting was in charge of book returns. "What a fortunate day for you as I've brought a spare with me for some beach reading." Professor Thrall dipped below the lip of the tub and returned with a massive black textbook that could be substituted for an anchor.

"Hold your arms out firm, dearie!" She shouted, but the book was already hurtling towards my unprepared twig arms. Physical education was not part of homeschooling.

Charlie snatched it from the air centimeters before my arms would have simply said no, thank you, and detached from my body. He held it out to me with ease as if it were no more than a pamphlet.

Pale green skin, under fangs, and unparalleled strength. Charlie was the politest, and the first, ogre I had met.

In a humble attempt at thanks, I grasped the heavy metal handle and held the door open for Charlie, using more strength than I'd care to admit. Most of the class had already filed into their seats in the crescent-shaped classroom that would have resembled a dungeon with its rigid stone walls and slightly damp floor if not for the eccentric decor. Tarot cards waddled through the air above as if they were on a morning stroll. Bookbags hung on the colored glass bottles stuck to the walls. A turquoise tube suctioned to the back wall wiggled with excitement as Charlie looped his bag around it. In the center of it all stood a wide mirror that reflected the rows of wooden desks in front of it, but not the children sitting in them.

"I've never seen an enchantment on a mirror like that," I remarked aloud.

"Oh, that isn't a mirror. That's the Looking Glass," Charlie replied. I raised an eyebrow, but Charlie had already started into the room.

With a forgetful hand, I let go of the door, which slammed shut mischievously, reverberating a low rumble throughout the room that snapped everyone's attention towards me.

"Blythe!" Melsella whisper-shouted from her chair, tapping the empty seat to the left of her excitedly. To her right sat a boy with a smirking smile.

That morning, Melsella had bombarded me with questions about my life on our way to breakfast (and all throughout it). While she spoke very fast, it was nice to have someone ask, despite the fact the most interesting information I had to tell about myself was that I had a webbed toe until I jammed my foot—a little too hard.

Melsella's attention flung to my right and her eyes widened in horror at the sight of Charlie beside me.

"BUM!" The Bell sounded once.

"If time is money, you just saved a dime!" A spirited voice rang from behind the Looking Glass. A slender person clothed in iridescent robes crossed in front of the classroom. From their coral skin, lavender and teal eyes, and pointed ears, Professor Sylmaris was a Curinquis—known for their curious behavior and manner of speaking, though I found their contortion of idioms quite refreshing from the drab wording of the creaturology textbook my aunt found in the marketplace.

Charlie and I slid into our seats in the last row as Melsella's eyes remained fixed on us with unwavering horror. The boy to her right's smirk delved into a grimace.

"A fresh and newly plucked student has joined us today. Please do not bite her as you are not bears and it isn't lunchtime yet," The Professor nodded seriously. "We are only a few weeks into our lesson, so would anyone fill Miss Seraphin up? Preferably to the brim, please."

Melsella's hand shot up, levitating her slightly from her chair with the gesture

"Oh, wonder-filled! Thank you, Miss Melsella, but I *see* Mr. Charlie is seated next to Miss Seraphin. The world is your oyster, Mr. Charlie!" Professor Sylmaris declared, motioning for him to fill me up (to the brim).

Charlie's jacket rumpled as he shrunk into his shoulders at the sight of everyone's stares. Some of the eyes I recognized from the hallway, but they now protruded mockery and seeped disgust. Ever since Professor Norwood had told me not everyone felt others' emotions, I had been practicing identifying the sensation to the emotion.

The night prior, I was walking through the foyer to go to my room when something coarse scraped against me. Sitting in a leather chair beside the staircase was a student hunching over a textbook. *Stress*, I realized. As I walked up the stairs, I became aware of that subtle rigidity everywhere. I wasn't too surprised. It was a school after all. Though, the texture of that same stress varied between the mythical and monstrous halls. One felt like a constant, familiar itch from the same people. The same small group. A family, maybe? The latter's was of a much larger weight. It was familiar in a different way. The same attack by different people. Unlike the mythical students, it wasn't in the intention they would do better.

Charlie, being an ogre, lived in that heavy hall. Was I sensing him last night? No. That was too much weight for one person to carry. It had to be. I couldn't tell if I was comforted or unsettled by that fact knowing Dante and Gus resided there too.

THE SON OF MARA

As classroom -66 stared at him, distress whirled around Charlie's head.

"O-occultism is the study of the s-s-supernatural," Charlie stuttered, eyes slipping to peering faces. I glared at them. A few people caught my distaste and decided the wall was a much better place to look. "While the word occult has been defined in many different ways over the years," His words gained balance. "Professor Sylmaris' class focuses on those variations and the different ways of viewing the supernatural as seen throughout time and continents."

"Knowledge is moving backwards and forwards for you, Mr. Charlie. Well done. Now!" Professor Sylmairs clapped their pink hands together, sending sparks into the atmosphere that then fell like shooting stars. The Looking Glass' silver surface intensified as if readying itself. "Since the founding of Esalroth by Headmaster Delacroix—who lived to the ripe age of two hundred and twenty-three and one quarter," With the Professor's words, the mirror showed a stout person in a grey robe surveying the very classroom we sat in, but it looked like it had yet to be fully set up yet. According to the mirror's reflection, dead and buried Headmaster Delacroix stood two rows ahead of where I sat. I flicked my eyes towards the spot, but no Headmaster stood there. *The mirror must reflect what has happened in this room*, I marveled.

"The Academy has taught all sorts of species from the centaurs in the west," the Looking Glass swirled like the syrupy iridescence of a bubble mixture and revealed a child with brown horns coiling on the sides of their head. Tan skin reached down to their torso before chestnut fur spread out to their backside supported by four hoofed feet. They appeared closer to the front of the classroom and looked to be giving a presentation.

"To the nymphs from above and below." The seats where Melsella and the boy were sitting were replaced by two children. One had blue skin that crystalized on their scalp to form a web of dew over their head. The other appeared to have the fluffiest of clouds for hair. The two children covertly slid notes to one another as they giggled, forgetting their misbehavior would be forever on replay for decades to come.

"Each student comes with their own culture that has their own ideas on the supernatural. Just as you all do. In quadruplets, please discuss your heritage and its beliefs regarding the occult."

"Would-d you like to be—" Before Charlie could finish the rest of his sentence, his words were swallowed by the ever-pleasant voice of Melsella.

"Blythe! You must join Bayle and I's group," She smiled, fixing her brown eyes away from Charlie as if she had not—or didn't care to—hear him. I considered the boy—Bayle—with his tan skin and contrastingly bright blonde hair. Something about him shined like the false gleam of counterfeit jewelry.

"Well, that makes only three in your group, so Charlie should join too," I said. Before Melsella could start her protests, I scraped my chair closer to them, signaling to form a circle. Reluctantly, the rest of them did the same. Melsella and Bayle kept their chairs at an apparent distance from Charlie, but he seemed to want the same, if not more, space.

"I'll go first," I declared, attempting to dissipate the tension. "I was born and raised here in Northern France as a witch. I was homeschooled, so I had to find most of the readings myself, but I read as much as I could about every place I had heard of. From what I've learned, I feel the supernatural is very real, but can also be conjured, or even summoned, by our own minds," I stated, feeling very eloquent in my assertion. As the group *listened* to what *I* had to say—as if *I* was a teacher—I was bolstered with empowerment. *What have I been missing?* I smiled to myself.

"Interesting," said Bayle. "I come a little way down from Mount Olympus. Svarog, Slavic god of fire and smithing—though some call him the true creator," Bayle winked at me. "Is my father. He taught me that demons are the personification of our own weakness. If you have a ghost in your house, maybe it is because you are too cowardly and need to be strengthened. Or disposed of." His teeth seemed to glisten brighter.

"That's not what I—" I started.

"I was raised *on* Mount Olympus," Melsella interjected. "For a short while. Athena herself taught me in her spare time." Melsella said proudly. Bayle sniffed.

I turned to Charlie who returned to the hunched pose I first met him in. "Where are you from, Charlie?"

Keeping his eyes down, Charlie replied, "Just n-north—I mean, south of here. In the bogs."

Melsella and Bayle eyed one another. Ignoring them, I continued on. "So, what did you learn about the occult there?"

"Um, well," Charlie shifted in his chair. "I didn't really ha-ave anyone to teach me. I actually taught myself to write before I cam to Esalroth, but, I like to read too." He looked at me in a way that treasured the company. "Maybe they're—the s-supernatural… things—aren't born evil. Maybe… we project our fears onto them b-because we don't understand them. Maybe they're demonized by us."

Melsella made a contemptuous humming noise. "So you think Hades, a god who reaps souls, is demonized by humans?"

The Charlie I had just met must have become just as entangled in the uncommon phenomenon of having someone listen to him as I was when he said: "Hades does his job. Zeus seems to only pursue uninterested nymphs."

Melsella clutched the grey fabric of her dress over her heart as she gasped so intensely, I could have sworn, for a fraction of a second, she inhaled all the oxygen in the atmosphere. "How dare you speak of the ruler of Olympus that way!"

Charlie shrunk, remembering the boy who he had been in the hall. Melsella jumped to her feet, clenching her fists at her side. Her gaze intensified with each harrowing second she stared at Charlie, and I feared if she could, she might suck every particle of air from his lungs.

After an excruciatingly still moment more, she turned around, gathered her things, and fluttered to a desk across the classroom. Bayle's chair scratched the floor as he stood. He collected his books but didn't leave until he bent down to Charlie, not a lock of his daring to slip from its precisely combed shape, and said, "At least people will remember Zeus. Can you say the same?"

Charlie shriveled as Bayle sauntered away.

"Charlie, I—" Words seemed to be too insignificant to mend the cruelty I had a disquieting suspicion came from a long lineage. "That was a horrible thing to say."

His gaze remained slumped on the floor as a whirlwind of anxiety kicked up around him again. Not in a storm, but that cruel period after where you can't avert your eyes from the wreckage.

I inched closer, carefully. "Is being remembered the same as being loved, though?"

"I wouldn't know," he replied. The collar of his jacket now concealed his chin while he huddled further into it. The variety of the people at Esalroth came from all over and under, but a common similarity throughout was their well-made attire—Melsella's frilly dresses, Gus' fine suit, Clyde's slick heels, Dante's fitted vest. The knitted sensation bridging Charlie and I felt akin to the miscounted stitching of Aunt Esther's attempted scarves. A homely kind of imperfect.

"There is still time to learn." I placed my hand on his shoulder as solace rippled through the stitches of his sleeve.

Charlie and I returned our chairs to our desk while Professor Sylmaris drifted from group to group.

"You must see a lot of cool creatures in the bogs," I said.

"Uh, yeah. I like the beetlbies," he replied.

I raised a brow as my entomology studies resurfaced in my mind. One would think beetlbies scaled backs would be protective against the volatile climate of the bogs. However, their scales are the darkest shade of black recorded in any creature, making heat their number one predator.

"But beetlbies—"

"Season's greetings!" Professor Sylmaris chimed. "How are you getting along, Miss Seraphin? If you find yourself trudging instead of skipping, my door is always open until dinner."

"Oh, thank you, Professor," I replied.

"Any and all time!" Professor Sylmaris exclaimed, making their way to the next group.

The rest of my classes—alchemy, areas of lucid dreaming, Prehistoric geography, and seasonal zoology—went well. Though I was more up to speed than my Professors' anticipated, I still had much more to learn, which excited me all the more. Answering the questions I could and giving insight on observations, my knowledge unspooled from the tight coil it had lain, only having itself for company. I enjoyed the silence in the room as people heard what *I* had to say. Me! Blythe Seraphin from the cottage in Northern France in the *country countryside*. Though I worried my classmates' nodding and affirmations were partially due to my... notable... status—one that I realized was not just due to the prophecy, but my father, the miracle worker. Despite being rivers and mountains away, he still had found a way to remind me I was his before my aunt's.

As the Bell rang to signal the end of classes, I couldn't stop picking at my cuticles. Bouncing from foot to foot, excitement and apprehension buzzed through me, clashing on who would prevail in my first training session with Professor Norwood in approximately five minutes.

CHAPTER 11

"You're late," Professor Norwood said as I panted through the door into the back courtyard.

"Yes, I'm sorry, Professor. It's these halls. They seem to have a mind of their own," I rasped, exhausted from my trek that only came to an end when I caved and signed a leprechaun's notebook in exchange for directions.

"They will grow accustomed to you eventually." The Professor winked.

My boots scuffed against the cobblestone ground as I sidled towards Professor Norwood. The rich green vines twisted down the walls that encased three sides of the courtyard. The fourth side opened up to the thick woods that must be frequented for nature explorations as a few beaten paths diverged in different directions.

"Alright. Show me what you can do," The Professor took a seat on one of the carved benches inside the courtyard that were waiting for students to sit and study, lay and rest, or—their assumed favorite—trifle and gossip. Fortunately for them today, they would be receiving quite a spectacle.

Okay, Blythe, just…, My mind blanked. *Just do… something.*

I placed my backpack on the ground in front of me and took a few steps back. Raising my hand towards it, I curled my fingers and thought really hard about lifting it. *Really* hard.

Nothing.

"I can do this. I can do this," I amped myself up, shaking out my shoulders and wringing my hands. The late September air of the afternoon seemed unable to decide if it was hot or cool.

I gripped the air firmer and thought *really, really* hard about lifting my backpack.

I frowned. If possible, my backpack laid even more still.

"I'm just gonna try something else!" I called to the Professor, who gave a thumbs up. I shuffled closer to the bag, staring at it intently. I thrust both hands forward and hurled them upwards, tearing through the air with all my might.

An ant started to crawl over the corpse known as my backpack.

"I, um, I think I'm doing something wrong," I reckoned.

"What did you do when you lifted the jewelry hand?" Professor Norwood asked.

"Nothing really. I wasn't even thinking about it."

Professor Norwood crossed her legs, revealing her black boots, slick with the afternoon sun. "That is an option to try."

"How am I supposed to not think about something?"

"I am as new to your abilities as you are, Miss Seraphin. If not more so. I can be your support, but you will have to be your own guide," she replied with ease that wafted through the clefts of stone and nooks of the vines. I reached out, its buttery texture marinating my palm as it warmed in my hands. I opened my grip, letting it melt through the air towards my backpack. As it became bathed in the milky substance, I became aware of its form, its gravity, which felt as airy as sweet cream.

"Well done, Miss Seraphin," The Professor broke me from my trance as she gazed up at my backpack, now hovering like a bird in waiting.

The snap of pride I felt was quickly swallowed by a deep gulp. The incident at home was not just a fluke. The students of Esalroth were not misled. And the Headmaster was not wrong.

I possessed unheard of magic. Magic that very well could be the opposing force to the Son of Mara.

The Professor walked toward me, her cape swaying. "How did that feel?"

My tongue held in my mouth as the backpack dropped to the ground. Connecting with what flowed from others unveiled another layer to the murmurs I pretended I couldn't hear. And it only felt like the surface of the whispers. Whispers I could not decipher the contents of just yet— nor did I know if I wanted to as it felt equally opportune at being a shy compliment or a ghastly secret.

"Good," I replied. "Nice."

"Nice? Hm," Professor Norwood studied me. "How did you accomplish feeling so nice?"

"My spirit again," I looked down at my hands that still felt slick with margarine. "It—I—felt your um… chillness."

The Professor held her hand to her chest with a laugh, a richly relaxed sound like hot cocoa on a night that wasn't cold enough to earn it. On her pinky finger, a singular silver ring lit up with sunlight. It was so thin it might have snapped if too much force were applied. "My chillness? Well, thank you, Miss Seraphin. Though, I am afraid some of the other students may not agree that I am so lenient in the classroom."

"So, what next?" I asked.

"Whatever you wish." The Professor assumed her position on the bench again. I almost suggested we play cards, but I was beginning to think too highly of the Professor for such weak attempts at stalling our training—though she probably would have offered a laugh.

THE SON OF MARA

Cautiously at first, I commanded stray pebbles to circle one another in the air like a Ferris wheel with the Professor's bubbling, pleased attitude. As I continued further, her intrigue twirled around me, nudging me to do more.

I took a paper and pencil from my backpack and wrote a letter without even touching the pencil. My anxious thoughts were slowly being triumphed by Professor Norwood's radiation of satisfaction that felt akin to shade on a summer's day. As I unlaced my boots and directed them to do a jig, my spirit swirled in an inner golden light, extending to my every joint and muscle, willing me to go farther for that release. And a release is what it was. My every seam unwound from the cramped position I maintained them in to keep myself from what I thought was a mistake, a defect. Could it be a good thing? Could I be a good thing?

I pulled my boots back on, ready to ask the benches to take flight, but the Professor called to me. "Try using *your* feelings this time."

I gave her a puzzled look. "What for? I'll always have an opponent to draw from."

"Fighting is not the sole purpose of your powers," Professor Norwood corrected.

"Well, isn't that why you all are so excited to have me here? I doubt everyone would be so…enthusiastic… if I wasn't going to save them all," I laughed, though it came out hollow.

Professor Norwood considered my statement for a moment. "What about after you save us all?"

After? I yearned to go places and meet people. I knew that much. But where was "places"? And who were people?

I shook my head free of the thought. "That's a long way away." *I hope.* "For now, I think I'll just…" I skipped towards the fountain and pulled water droplets over my head with the Professor's plain sleet of consideration. "Soak it all in." The droplets fell over my head like my very own rainstorm. Not enough to drench me, but enough to cause my baby hairs to curl.

Refreshed and more rejuvenated than I had felt in years, I noticed the clock cemented high in the courtyard's wall. A black like deep marble formed its face while its numbers and hands gleamed gold. Pulling my backpack together, I said, "Sorry, Professor." I brushed my hair down with my fingers. "I've got to meet someone for… studying."

CHAPTER 12

I found Dante at the height of a varnished wooden ladder in the library, balancing on his toes while stretching himself out to a grey book he almost had a hold on. As he attempted to advance toward the book, desperation pressurized the distance from the tips of his fingers to the spine they were inches from grazing. Urgency caught my wrists when his rashness peaked, unbalanced. If he twisted any further, he most surely would fall. Though the book was farther and higher than what I had just attempted in the courtyard, I jolted my hand upwards, wrapping the uncomfortable pressure around my knuckle like a beaten leather strap, and gave a firm tug. The book collapsed to the floor and Dante stayed firm on the ladder.

I took a relieved breath, dissipating the fear knotted in my shoulders. I had actually did it and it was almost... easy.

"Started without me?" I asked, slinging my backpack over an orange lounge.

"Well, now I know I shouldn't have," Dante replied, scaling down the ladder, placing his hands on his knees when he met the ground. I could feel the gratitude bubble in him, finally having the sturdy floor beneath his feet.

I assessed the distance from the portrait of the lady and her burning books to the final shelf. Even though Dante was almost a quarter of the way through, we had quite a journey ahead of us.

As Dante heaved up the gigantic ladders, I boasted a little as I pulled books from the highest shelves without leaving the carpet. Although, due to the difference in their sizes, I struggled to concentrate and wrap my magic around more than one book at a time.

Abandoning my playful bragging in favor of efficiency, I joined Dante on another ladder, scouring for titles of possible relevance. The books I found varied from thin cloth bounds to dusted leatherbacks that must have been born from the same bulky lineage as my occultism textbook. Some of the texts just barely fit within what Dante considered "Mara material". Anything relating to demons, curses, monsters, and everything else of the sort fit the drastically wide bill of possibility.

Dante and I had to assemble our bottomless collections on two separate lacquered tables while we mulled over their pages. The library seemed to huddle in closer to get a peek of what we were reading. Determination surged through my veins, and I wondered whether I was using magic or sheer will to pursue the ceaselessly dense passages. Pricks of candlelight from the candelabras attending to the tables grew brighter as the sun crouched closer to the horizon.

Too soon, Dante slammed his final book dramatically onto the pile next to him. "Done."

I peered up from my heap of open books, all read through to varying degrees. My head ached from reading the elementary penmanship of people considered to be scholars. I felt as though their crude scratches coiled around my cornea as my eyes pulsed.

"Find anything?" I asked, cracking my back.

Dante, eyes as refreshed as the first waking of nightfall, replied, "Nothing new. Every account has a different perspective on her. Her son could be anything from a gargantuan demon to a fire-breathing beetle."

I hauled a stack of books over to Dante's table, comparing my findings to his. There had to be something we were missing, a connection hidden in the throws of dust and barely legible script. But Dante was right. Depictions of her ranged from jagged scrawls of a monstrous beast that looked so hastily drawn I feared they were sketched moments before she devoured the artist to neatly brushed lines that formed a perfectly normal woman—except for her eight splotchy red eyes and the severed head clutched in her taloned grasp.

"Wait," I eyed two books at opposite corners of the table. I scampered towards them, throwing their covers over. As I read their titles and authors, something plucked like a taut string in my beaten mind. A common thread strung through a sewing needle— thin, but there, nonetheless. I turned to the other books strewn across the table, frantically combing over the pages of cord journals, polished hardbacks, and tattered soft covers, comparing countries, and cultures. Dante was right that each culture had a different impression of Mara.

But those same cultures' depictions varied throughout time.

"Dante, look." He leaped from his seat, searching between the two books I held open. "A Slavic practitioner wrote this book in 200 BC and shows Mara looking like this." I pointed to a painted image of a woman with six legs, six arms, and six heads that had "destroyer of lands" inscribed on the side. "But this one —written by a Slavic philosopher one hundred years ago—shows Mara as..." I pointed to a journal that contained a portrait of a woman with no limbs at all who slithered around like an undead snake from the bottomless pits of hell.

"The same places depict Mara in vastly different ways over time," I continued, speaking quicker as the thread began to unwind faster, clearer. "Maybe *that* is her power. She's able to change forms and conjure the suitable weapon, whether that's a ball of fire like in ancient China." I gestured to a textbook that showed Mara towering over entire buildings while setting them ablaze. "Or demon dogs like in renaissance Greece." I pointed to another. "Or elemental manipulation, like right here in France just half a century ago." I gestured to the final textbook that depicted Mara as a hauntingly frail spirit with a mouth disjointed wide enough to consume a person whole.

"Gods below," Dante gaped, unable to avert his eyes from the books baring their souls across the table.

"I know…"

I couldn't look away either. The unsettling realization dawned on me like an unwelcome morning.

Dante sank down in his chair, causing its legs to whine, and rubbed the knot in his forehead, pained that he had to ask the obvious. "How do we find someone who can change shape?"

I dissected the books we'd taken out, trying to untangle the thread that had dragged us to a frustrating knot. I dug my fingers in, refusing to let go. I was *the one*. I racked my brain harder, bolstered by the humming in my veins I unearthed with Professor Norwood just hours ago. I refused to be that easily bested by a demon, not after I felt the cusp of my power. The bare beginnings of what would save everyone from such a heinous stain on the world. It would save *me* from a life of waiting for him to strike. If I could find and defeat him, Aunt Esther wouldn't be so fearful of me seeing the world. Doing this would save me from a life lived only knowing the four walls of a cottage.

After a moment, the knot didn't give way completely, but it gave enough.

"We'll focus on the most recent accounts," I said, holding up the ghastly drawing of Mara from a French explorer half a century ago. "And we'll see where that gets us."

Dante eyed our trail of books. There was a mound of them, but they all contained only a page or two on Mara herself. Narrowing down our search to anything recent would strip us even more. What could be considered recent when talking about an immortal demon was equally as foiling.

Dante's face sighed deeply, shadowed in contemplation. I braced for his response that this was too much. It was too hard. He had other things to do. He was sorry, but this was a waste of time.

He fidgeted with the corner of a burgundy book. "Alright, do you want to come here after dinner then?"

My shoulders released as relief flooded my body. Though Melsella was my official guide to Esalroth, Dante felt like an escort through the invisible layer of Esalroth. Not just on how to make friends, but feel comfortable around them. Not just on how to learn, but understand—in academics and… other things.

A faint smile flickered on my lips. "Yes, that's—that's a good idea." His dark eyes wavered on me until red bloomed in his brown cheeks and he glanced away. I pretended not to notice, saying, "But when is—"

"Bum, bum, bum," The Bell sang. I looked up at the ceiling and smiled as if the Bell had anticipated my grumbling stomach, and moved time just a little quicker.

CHAPTER 13

My boots strolled lighter over the polished floors of Esalroth as Dante, and I made our way to the dining room. The anxious mass festering in my chest since I laid eyes on the academy's black gates had subsided to a memory. I was *in* *Esalroth*. Friends were within reach and my power was not worthy of concern but accepted. Praised. My spirit felt like it was starting to settle into the limits of my skin.

After I slightly alluded to my traveling aspirations, Dante's whole being perked as upright as a fed flower. Enthusiasm buzzed from the bottoms of his feet to his tuft of black hair that looked like a writer's candlelit ink under the warm lamps lining the halls. As we rounded corners I patted myself on the shoulder for recognizing, Dante rambled about books that's pages practically smelled of the water of the Nile or ice of the Arctic. Each word depicting a hidden experience of worlds near and far. His voice twinkled the same as a dying star as he recalled the accuracy of a piece about Taiwan.

He peppered me with questions about the ideal climate, my opinions on the constant buzz of city life or the boundless quiet of the country, and whether I would prefer to constantly smell raw fish or cow manure.

The flicker of strangeness I felt at such questions I quickly, and whole-heartedly, embraced. No one had indulged my dreams before or gone so far as to recommend how to fulfill them. The spark of an idea, however, I instantly extinguished. I mean, how absurd would it be to travel with Dante after graduating from Esalroth?

Just how absurd? We'd only just met, after all.

Yet, I felt like I would know him for ages to come.

Dante finished telling me how I might have some difficulty in the country as there was not much access to those sweet, sweet processed treats out there. I hastily reminded him I was *from* the country, which all the more proved his point.

With no more finesse than this morning's occultism class, I heaved the cafeteria door open for Dante, who nodded his head in gracious thanks. As my arms pinched me to let go of the door before my tendons snapped, Dante halted.

"Oh no," he groaned.

"What? What's wrong?" I let go of the black iron knob, supporting the door with my body instead. I faced the inside of the dining hall where students bustled around from table to table, carting entrees and drinks of every sort. Seated at the front row of tables, the elf child reached up to a minotaur who handed the child a bowl of cereal that looked comically small in his hands. To the left, plates clattered against each other as a short person in all black tossed them onto the table of unsuspecting students. *Gus?*

A burst of wind blew so forcefully over my shoulders my sand-colored dress swished upwards. For a moment, I feared Melsella stood behind me, ready for me to congratulate her on that funny joke. Thankfully, the gust descended from a person with the snout and wings of a bat that flew above Dante and I to deliver more food on a tray from an unknown kitchen.

"You're late, Shyung," the person called back as they flapped into the room.

I turned to Dante, brushing my misplaced hair out of my face. "Are we all playing pretend restaurant? I must inform you I left my wooden bread and plastic pasta at home."

He sighed, scrubbing a tired hand over his face. Eyes still fixed on the clamors of students complaining their orders were mixed up, he explained, "The last Tuesday of the month is when all the Chucks—er, I mean, Chaunceys—get cleaned and refurbished. So, the students take turns serving and cooking the meals. First up are the monstrous students."

I shivered, trying to digest the word. *Monstrous*. How disgusting that word could be attributed to children. The word twisted cruelly into my heart even more being associated with Dante. Thoughtful Dante who said my indecision about his questions meant I was a true traveller, destined to journey to every wonder that caught my eye.

That word should be reserved for one person and their wicked heir only.

He turned to me. "I'm sorry, but I'll have to stay and clean the dishes after, especially for being so late. Can we meet tomorrow in the library?"

"Oh, yeah, no. Don't worry about—"

Gus dumped three full platters into Dante's hands. He fumbled to keep hold of them all, and I sprung forward to support the third from tipping. Gus was aware Dante had only two arms (it would be pretty hard to mistake him for Clyde) but did not care.

"Table nine," Gus instructed. Even under his full suit and thick mask, his annoyance felt like barbed wire. "Give the one with straw hands their food last. They poked my mask." As Gus humphed away, I swore I saw something crawl up his pant leg. It didn't seem to bother him.

Dante said his goodbyes, and I was left with a gilded pond of satin colored lily pads, all with faces I only recognized in passing or impromptu notebook signing.

All except one.

Melsella and Bayle's.

I strided over, forcing myself to breathe and smile. *Breathe and smile.* I could pretend for half an hour. I *had* to pretend if I wanted to eat.

Usually, I wouldn't have minded skipping a meal or even snagging a stray roll from one of the plates as the "waiters" whisked them around. Aunt Esther's reluctance to go to the marketplace made pickings very slim by the end of the month, and I learned to live off portions fractions of the ordinary size. But exercising my magic unearthed an insatiable hunger.

Before I could see the dishes, their delicious scents travelled up my nose and plunged into my hollow stomach. Each silver platter seemed to be dripping like the saliva of a hungry beast. At that point, steak, cereal, or an unholy mix of both sounded appetizing. Anything to disperse the hardened grumbles in my stomach.

As we made eye contact, Melsella's ruffled dress flapped while she waved me over. The corner of Bayle's mouth turned upward in a lazy smirk. Each feature of his contradicted the other. His blinding blonde hair. His deeply sun-tanned skin. His pure white teeth. His anvil grey suit. Yet, they all engaged each other because Bayle demanded it.

I pulled the red cushioned dining chair out, and Melsella watched me excitedly while Bayle eyed me hungrily. It unnerved me at the thought it could be for something other than food.

"Hey, Melsella," I said, flattening my dress. "Bayle," I nodded.

"Oh, Blythe. I'm so sorry. You just missed orders," her grey curls bounced while she poured her complete sorrow for me into each word. "But Bayle ordered a rather large meal. I'm sure he wouldn't mind sharing. Right, Sigmis?" She looked at him with doe eyes and a smile that dared him to contradict the answer she had in mind.

Sigmis—as I assumed that was his first name—slowly traced his brown eyes, as sharp as carved wood, from my waist up. Want undulated from him like a wave of dense humidity. "Certainly not," he winked. Every cell in me was just about ready to reject itself as his eyes became more pent up with desire. His watchfulness was the most unbearable I had endured yet.

At least you're getting fed for it.

"There you are!" A cheerfully unmistakable voice squealed from behind me. I suppressed a smirk at Melsella and Bayle's disturbed composures before I got up to pull the chair out next to me for Clyde. The mythical students weren't just being served. So were the magical. *Thank the goddesses above.*

"Oh, how chivalrous you are, Bly," Clyde cooed while she tucked her laced black dress underneath her, then she settled into the chair. "I'll have to ask you to escort me to the Hallow's Eve Ball."

I cocked my head, and Melsella countered, "That's a month away."

"I know! How will I ever fashion a dress in time?" Clyde exclaimed, throwing all her hands in the air, causing her straight black hair to tumble over her back.

"You… you make your own dresses?" Bayle snickered at Melsella's question, mistaking what slipped from her widened eyes as disgust. Only I could tell it was the short pull of fascination.

"Oh, of course! It took me months after I came out of my cocoon to discover such things as shops. By then, only the clothes I created myself suited my taste. That, and it's hard to find clothes with four arm holes." She extended out her arms and glided her fingers over the sleeves that draped lower at the wrists. Everything was precisely sewn and enchantingly inspired from the frilly neckline to the criss-crossed laces across the bodice . I could only imagine how long it took her to forge such an elaborate dress, though I assumed having four arms offered some help.

Melsella's eyes travelled across the seams, admiring each like the careful strokes of a portrait.

"Aw, look at her face," Bayle interrupted, staring at me with a fake pout. "I don't think Blythe has been told about the ball yet."

Melsella snapped back on the overly excited smile that only now I could tell was aching after it was put alongside Clyde's natural energy. What for—or because of—I didn't know.

"The Hallow's Eve Ball is a tradition at Esalroth. It takes place every year on Halloween and you're expected to dress like a formally dressed version of yourself," Melsella nodded, angling her chin upwards.

I raised an eyebrow, and Clyde swooped in, yellow eyes the color of buttercups. "It's to celebrate us and who we are." Clyde looked around as students clopped and soared. Children with feathers sat next to those with fur. Friends smiled as one of them refilled all their glasses with only their palms. A celebration of the mythical, magical, and monstrous.

"E-excuse me," a voice quavered from behind me. In his limp blue jacket, Charlie balanced platters in his hands, keeping them from slipping by tucking them in the crooks of his elbows. His fangs quivered, and I couldn't discern if it was from the concentration of keeping the plates stabilized or the character of the people he was serving.

Charlie laid down the entire tray on the table. He must not have been the person who took their order and didn't know who had what. Melsella took her tilapia without the slightest acknowledgment to Charlie, leaving three plates behind. One consisted of potato pancakes and the other pirogies. Realizing they were both Slavic dishes, I wondered if Bayle was a little homesick too. On the final plate was lamb encrusted in a thick char and doused in a light brown sauce.

I waited for Bayle to take his pick of which of the *three* meals he forced his peers to cook, but his bleached brows caved into a scowl. He snatched the third plate, dangling it in front of him with one hand.

"Is this supposed to be funny? Charring my lamb because, what? I'm a fire god? Ha-ha, real good comeback," Bayle sneered with a presumptuous air, but I felt the agitation ticking away in him.

"I-I didn't m—I didn't cook the f-foo—," Charlie stammered. His jacket seemed to consume him.

"Whatever, ogre. Just bring me a new one," he carelessly tossed the plate onto the tray, slumping back and crossing his arms over his tailored suit. His recklessly arrogant attitude propelled the dish just past the edge of the tray, causing it to plunge to the ground. I lunged forward, catching it by the face as it hurtled upside down. The gruff charcoal mixed unceremoniously with sauce against my hand, making me feel like I was touching slimy paint chips. It probably would have been smarter to just use my powers, but they hadn't become as much of a reflex as I would have liked them to be yet

I turned the plate right side up and placed it back on the tray, detaching my hand from the burned and drowned lamb. Beige sauce and flakes of charcoal coated my hand, and Clyde immediately took hold of it, ignoring the napkins in front of us in favor of the availability of her own sleeve to wipe away the mess.

I jerked my hand away. "Clyde! You'll ruin your dress!"

She fanned me off. "I can make others."

Bayle seized my wrist, his lazy eyes lolling over me. "Do you know what kind of sauce this is? It's oochmielle. One of the last recipes my mother made before she left this world when I was only a tot." He rubbed his thumb over my veins as his eyes pretended to reminisce, unaware of the fact I could feel the deviousness forging the facade. He looked into my eyes with a coveting shade of brown. "Gods rest her soul. She would hate to see me let such perfect sauce go to waste." He eyed my palms, estimating them. "Especially on such a fine dish."

Before I could process the shrinking distance between us, his tongue was slavering over my hand, licking up the sauce with a caress. His firm grip squeezed into my bones, wanting to know every part of a new possession.

I yanked my hand away and slapped him square across his cheeks, extinguishing the desire from his soiled eyes, smearing the remaining sauce across his face. Even for hitting with my left, Bayle was hunched over, clutching the aggravated red side of his face, reminding me of the way the boy from the marketplace fell when the pieces of rock scratched. Like no one had ever dared to lay a finger on him before.

I was beginning to hate blondes.

Dante marched up, assessing the scene consisting of a frazzled Bayle and a stunned table. "What's going on over here?"

It took me a moment to take into account how the slap reverberated through my palm, and most definitely, the room. Dozens of green, blue, brown, and violet eyes encircled our table.

"Wouldn't you like to know, Shyung. I see you holed up in the library for hours with her. What did you tell her about me then, huh? That you can't take a joke?" Disgust snaked through me at the fact Bayle attributed my disdain for him to the *possibility* of rumors rather than the revolting use of his dead mother to entice me.

"Dante is helping me research the Son of Mara. You know, the person I'm going to save you from. Though, I'm considering letting him get a nip at you now," I shot back.

Bayle's eyes upended themselves, rage spewing from him as he whipped his head to me. "You're letting this freak help you? Do you even know what he is?"

"Don't you call him that. Of course I know who he is," I rebutted, gritting my teeth.

Charlie placed a hand on Dante's stiffened shoulders.

"Sigmis...," Melsella cut in apprehensively.

"No, no. She of all people should know what we saw wash up to the gates four years ago. Your library assistant dared to come here with a mouth dripping with blood," Bayle hissed. Dante's gaze hardened against the floor, which only kicked out a barking laugh from Bayle. "Thank your gods Professor Norwood can pity people like you."

Charlie murmured something harsh under his breath as his red brows dug together.

"What did you say, ogre? Come on, say it louder, or did they not teach you how to speak in the bogs?" Bayle sniped.

Charlie went to speak, packed with the force of a caged lion, but was cut off by the snap of small fingers and the howl of a dog.

A blur of rusty fur bolted in between Dante and Charlie. Its black claws skittered across the polished stone before it pounced, revealing its skull head. A demon dog.

The dog's jagged indents in its skull—its teeth— clamped onto Bayle's pant leg, shredding his custom suit but not breaking the skin. The dog was latched onto him almost playfully. Bayle managed to kick off the creature with his other leg, sending its body sliding across the floor until it bumped into another table. A tense silence filled the room before it popped with the shrieks of students jumping from their seats. Silverware clattered to the floor as children hid behind columns and climbed on top of tables.

I darted my eyes around for the source of a portal. Demon dogs did not just roam around the world unless they were brought from hell. The only evidence I found was Gus giggling maniacally.

The past few days fell into place. The disappearing food. Mysterious bugs. Gus was an underworld summoner—and a young one too. Communicating and calling upon creatures from such a place was no easy feat, even for adults. The demon dog hadn't killed Bayle, which meant Gus had spent a year—*years*—training it.

Bayle clutched his tattered clothing in his hands, eyes blazing with fury.

"YOU!" Bayle shot up, thrusting his finger at Gus who just laughed harder, sounding like hard rain on a tin roof. Bayle reared his hand, raw hatred rattling in his every fiber. Suddenly, a sphere of fire erupted from his palm. A molten pit levitated in his hand as thin flames fanned upwards.

"No!" Clyde yelped.

Bayle chucked the ball of flames at Gus, but another boy dressed in black stepped in the way.

"Dante!" I cried, springing from my seat while Melsella clutched her chair in shock. Clyde seemed to breathe a sigh of relief. I could deal with Bayle's claims about Dante and Clyde's surprising lack of worry later. But, being raised by a healing witch, instinct drove me forward.

Dante's height saved his face from being scorched, but his white shirt had a rigid hole seared through it, its singed ends curling brown. Before I made contact with his shoulders, I was already contemplating how powerful a brew might be needed and mapping the fastest way home to retrieve any rarer ingredients.

I grabbed him, ripping away at the hand he was patting himself down with to analyze his burn—the curves of his exposed patch of skin smiled back at me as healthy as ever.

I retracted my hand back. "W-what? How is that…," I faltered. The heat flaring from Bayle's hand was enough to be felt from where I sat. Dante should have been doubling over in pain, but instead, he took my shoulder calmly.

"Will you walk me to my room?" He asked softly, face gentle.

"No, you need to go to the infirmary," I refuted. I turned to Clyde for support, but her yellow eyes had mellowed, leaving only pity.

"Blythe," the level of his voice did not change, but a new layer of assurance coated it. "Please trust me."

Protests surged through me, but a pang in my chest silenced them. *Trust me.* Bayle's terrifying accusations resounded in my mind. I searched through Dante for a flicker of beguilement. All I sensed in front of me were eyes so still, so sure. So accepting. But not necessarily of me. Of what he was choosing to do.

To confess.

CHAPTER 14

As teachers rushed to the dining hall, Dante and I slipped through the chaotic flow of curious students and ascended the foyer staircase. I had half a mind to sling my arm around Dante in case a rush of delayed pain crippled him, but he walked up the steps without so much as a hobble.

Puddles of apricot light dripped from the candlelit lamps onto the carpets of the three hallways. The ponds of orange glazed the blue mythical carpet and the magical violet carpet, inviting you to swim in their warmth as you yawned your way to bed. The light pooling on the deep red of the monstrous hall dared you to test if it was scorching.

I followed Dante down the crimson carpet. The candles seemed to be at their wit's end, causing the hall to grow darker the further we walked down, seemingly, never-ending. On each side, rows of sleek black doors faced one another, all entombed in dark wood. Etched onto each was not a golden symbol resembling the student inside, but numbers painted in grey.

66,597

66,598

We stopped at the door 66,599.

"There can't possibly be over sixty-six thousand students here," I stated, but Dante placed his hand on the brass doorknob and said, "There isn't. It's our student number. Since Esalroth's founding, I'm student 66,599."

"But the mythical students don't have their number written on their door."

"There's less of them, so there's no need when they're so notable, and so… good," he clarified while twisting the door open.

Grey charcoal walls contained the only furniture the room could fit: an iron-framed bed with a thin mattress and a simple chest. Dante managed to make the murkiness the room leaked less consuming by tacking a few famous paintings around. A stack of books sat like a skeletal spine beside his bed in a makeshift nightstand.

Dante took a seat on the chest, gesturing for me to take the bed. I perched on the side of it as it whined under my weight.

With only the pus-colored light of a simple lantern hanging beside the door, Dante's face was stroked by shadow.

"Bayle told you the truth. I entered Esalroth with the life of my last victim hanging from my lips. I was only eight."

I gulped down his naked words, clawing to keep the Dante of the past two days intact. The compassionate stranger who grounded me from a panic attack. The helpful acquaintance who offered to assist in the practically impossible task of researching an undetectable, immortal demon. The thoughtful person who I longed to call *friend* after he promised to show me all the books about different countries he could find. But just like in the dining hall, my healing instincts came to me first, reminding me Dante had the opposite impulses.

The only sentences I managed were, "You were eight? But Bayle said you came to Esalroth four years ago." My first assessment of Dante and his boyish curls and awkward fumblings made me assume he was my age.

"Yes, I did." He kept his gaze down, tracing the knuckles of his hands. "The majority of myths and folklore claim vampires stay the age they were turned in, but in actuality, we only retain that youth if we… feed." He gripped one hand with the other as if reliving a nightmare. "I was only eight when I turned so I—" He swallowed hard, clamping his eyes shut as he forced the words out. "I did what I thought I was supposed to. Then, after four years, I couldn't bare it anymore. So I travelled to Esalroth, and

Professor Norwood taught me how to exist benevolently." Dante breathed. "What a horrid thing to have to learn."

He shifted his weight as he continued. "She's helped me through the past four years as the age I pushed away by feeding came back in double. So now, at sixteen, I age one year at a time."

"Does… does that have anything to do with being a vampire?" I asked, pointing to his unscathed chest.

"Yes. Professor Norwood told me sunlight isn't the death sentence I was treating it as back in Taiwan. It only causes me to be wounded like a human would. It also causes me to… remember pain. So if I stepped out in the sun tomorrow, my chest would hurt like I had just been burned to the third degree yesterday." He planted his elbows on his knees as he clasped his hands together, bowing his head to the floor. "If you don't want to work with me—or," The following phrase he had to drag out from somewhere far deeper than his throat. "Or… talk anymore, I understand."

The horror rattling inside me was not due to the past he assumed, but the idea of a being child forced to endure the gruelling sensation of being transformed.

I could hide behind my self-righteous healing instincts and say I would never murder people if I was turned, but that was me *now*. What about me when I was only eight? Completely alone?

I shuddered at the thought and knelt down in front of him, placing my hand on his knee. "You protected Gus even after he was so curt with you the first time we met."

Dante looked at me, eyes the darkest shade of lamenting. "He's only a child. I'll swallow my pride to show him some kindness if it means he won't end up like me."

"Like you? He'd be lucky to be like you," I pressed.

"Gus has yet to murder anyone."

"Dante, you were only a child then too."

He lowered his eyes, my words washing over him like holy water. The bare beginnings of absolution.

"Come here. You are so cold," I said, situating myself next to him on the chest.

"I'm always cold," he replied.

"Well, now you are too cold," I humphed, wrapping my arms around him and taking his head in the crook of my neck. Bayle tried to drive a wedge between us by unveiling a version of Dante conjured in nightmares, but that version stood only as tall as the petrified little boy who had his life capsized. He chose to sacrifice the careless ease of succumbing to his impulses in favor of unlearning the harsh nature that was forced into his cells. Under my arm resting over his shoulder, I felt the tender hum of the Dante of the past and present, beginning to acknowledge one another without judgement. A simple nod to one another, at most, but a start.

I held him closer, noticing he smelled of the unabashed perfume of antique books, the gurgling of my stomach echoed through the sparse room. We pulled apart into a laughing fit.

"I think I have something for that," Dante said, standing. He offered his hand to me, looking at me with secretive eyes. I squinted at him playfully, my mouth twisted into a guessing smile when I accepted it. He bent down and unlatched the chest. Neatly folded clothes in primarily black—to attract any heat, I presumed —laid next to stacks of school papers, some stray pencils and erasers, and an absurd amount of hats. Situated on a heather gray sweater was the neatly tied bag of taffies from lunch.

CHAPTER 15

"Again!" Professor Norwood clapped encouragingly, but her enthusiasm only made me groan.

I struggled to shred a paper without the use of my hands in the courtyard's raw mid-afternoon sun. My skin crawled. I never noticed the demanding energy that crackled from the daylight until I had everything to do. Everything to be.

After double and triple-checking over Dante the night before, I returned back to my room far too late, staying up to goddessless hours to finish the homework I had forgotten all about. Melsella's clammy hands jostled me awake this morning. I felt like I had only slept a fraction of a wink.

"Come, come! It's only your second day. You can't fall behind yet," she said, though her words sounded strangely like my father's. I shook away his creeping presence. Eyes groggy, I stumbled in my haste, trying to slip my dress over my head with Melsella urging me to move faster.

"You might as well just float me to breakfast," I mumbled, suppressing a yawn as I rushed to pack my bookbag.

"Good idea!"

"Wait, wait—" A gust of wind wrapped around me from my shoulders to my toes. My feet dangled in the air as I clung to my bag. From this view, our room looked even *more* expansive than Dante's.

When my eyes, startled awake now, adjusted, I noticed Melsella's usual palette of grey and white attire was disrupted by a single purple bow sewn to her collar.

Noticing me eyeing it, Melsella clutched the decoration, leaving me to drop the foot or three to the floor.

"Just something I'm trying," she said timidly while she stroked it. Then, speaking in a nervous flurry, "I know my family's colors are grey and white, but it's such a little thing…" Her eyes widened while she searched my expression. "You don't think they'll mind, do you?"

Seeing Melsella so cautious wobbled the performatively exuberant impression I had of her. Operating under the world's— or family's—pressure was something I was starting to empathize with.

I shrugged. "Not unless they hate style."

Melsella's mouth quirked, and a feeling as warm as milk poured into tea flowed through her. I could tell that this smile, for the first time, was genuine.

"The Greeks practically invented art, thank you very much."

The rest of the day was not so breezy. Gossip of the event from last night ranged from partially true to absurdly unrealistic. Gus and Bayle managed to get off with only a week's detention after they collectively decided it was an accident—the details of this collaboration, hazy. Some people claimed Gus bribed Bayle to keep quiet and others swore a creature Gus summoned now possessed Bayle and would act as him until the end of time.

"Hey," I said to Gus in Prehistoric geography class. He gave me an indifferent stare in acknowledgement. "I made this for your um,... dog." I handed him a glass vile that contained a mixture of salt, vinegar, and lemon juice. Healing a creature of the underworld required ingredients that would hurt when applied to a human's wound.

He took the vile, then shook it. "It looks like pee."

"It's a healing elixir," I replied, scratching the back of my head. "I just thought after Bayle kicking it, and then colliding with the table it might have a few bruises."

He gave it a once over again before turning back to his assignment. "Thanks."

"No problem. I just wanted to say… well, it was really selfless what you did for Dante."

He whipped his head back to me. "Did—did Dante…

say that?" His grip tightened around his pencil as he stuttered to

cork the care he let leak out. "Er, I mean—did…"

"He cares for you very much," I said. Though I couldn't

see his face, Gus' shoulders lifted and his usually prickly feelings

felt more like a dull needle. He nodded and continued doing his

work.

As I drifted from alchemy to lucid dreaming to seasonal

creaturology in a daze, my peers bombarded me with questions

and, strangely, congratulations.

"You were so brave to stop the beast," one wide-eyed

fairy had whispered to me in class.

I smiled flatly, trying to keep my dwindling focus on the

assignment, sentences seemingly falling out of my brain as soon

as I finished the line.

"Yeah," a water nymph nodded. "Those monsters are

dangerous."

I glanced up from my work, cocking a brow at the

nymph. "You mean the demon dog, right?"

The nymph and fairy flashed a look at one another. The

nymph's eyes searched my agitated expression before answering:

"Um… yeah." They both turned back to their work.

I mulled over the encounter for the remainder of the

school day, not even attempting to lend so much as an ear to the

class discussion. Had they been referring to *Gus* as a monster? As much as I tried to hush the idea with reasoning such as other students never referring to one another as mythicals or magicals, one constant I could not deny—or ignore as the compliments followed me until I reached the solitude of the courtyard—was that people believed *I* had stopped the demon dog instead of Dante.

I had not done a single thing besides exist to win my peers' appreciation. The only explanation for Dante being robbed of his brave feat was the title he bore under the academy's name. *Monster.*

"Miss Seraphin?" Professor Norwood's voice ripped me from my mind, equal parts muddled with recollections of the day's concerning events and the weariness that seeped from my skull to my arms, lazily extended to the paper I was levitating.

"Yes, yes. Sorry, Professor. What were you saying?" It took a worrying amount of concentration to keep from yawning.

"I said, reflect back on when you broke up the rock," she repeated.

Bitter distaste furled in my stomach at the continuation of using that wretched boy as the source of my power. If I had to keep reliving that day to gain control of my powers, I was determined to master them quickly.

I tensed my arm, trying to wriggle the Professor's cream-like repose I used to hold up the paper into the atoms, but its silkiness only slipped through my fingers. I balled my dormant hand into a fist as if it could keep hold of the remaining patience and consciousness I possessed.

Giggles burst from the woods in front of me. Through the thickets, two children trampled over one another, playing. At first, annoyance brushed my insides like straw. My concentration would never hold if I had to deal with their cacklings. Then, I recognized the students. *The fairy and the nymph.* And they weren't just playing tag or hide-and-seek. No, they were playing pretend. The nymph tossed balls of water at the fairy, who had two pointy twigs stuck in their hair as they chased around the nymph—the fairy, growling, and barking, *like a dog.*

My annoyance bristled into indignation. How dare they? How dare they prance around as the "monsters" they so quickly, so openly despised. I glanced at Professor Norwood, tapping her foot while she waited for me to finish my demonstration. Her buttered ease sizzled in my hands, bubbling into a rage. The edges of the paper started to curl brown, withering away at the page while fire edged down it until a defiant scrap of its ashen remains swayed down to the floor.

I turned to the Professor, who, instead of oozing with satisfaction, stilled. Her face looked from me to the ash to the contents of her mind. Such an odd reaction took me sideways. I had used my *own* feelings, just like she wanted. Despite being faded by sleep, I converted my own anger into power. *Flaming power.*

I smirked to myself. Maybe I didn't have to be so worried about the Son of Mara after all.

"Bravo!" An elated voice called.

From behind us, Headmaster Tenold looked undone from his usual restrained demeanor. Radiant beams practically sparkled off of him. I warmed under them as I realized they weren't just satisfied. They were *exhilarated.*

"Miss Seraphin," The Headmaster hurried forward, taking my hand in his. "Your gift, it is remarkable. It is *extraordinary.*" He shook my hand, his cool grip eager in my hands.

Remarkable Blythe Seraphin. Not the sheltered, neglected daughter. Not the weird girl in the marketplace, barely able to afford a discounted item, nonetheless, a friend. *Extraordinary* Blythe Seraphin.

"Thank you, sir," I replied proudly.

Regressing back into himself slightly, he held his hands together, his white coat blinding in the sunlight. "Tomorrow, we shall hold a spectacle after school to demonstrate your powers."

"Wait, what?" I retracted back, and even Professor Norwood looked surprised.

"Miss Seraphin, you have no idea how long these students have been waiting for you. For assurance they will be able to live safely." As he spoke, his white hair remained still, as if nervous movement may disrupt the moment. I considered his idea. Standing in front of the entire academy to demonstrate powers that seemed to move at their own pace was a far cry from the card tricks I performed in the marketplace. But, as I stared into the Headmaster's tired blue eyes, I could see that the students were not the only ones needing reassurance.

"Only if foods are provided," I snapped a finger gun at him jokingly.

To my astonishment, he replied, "Name the horderves."

CHAPTER 16

"Sorry, sorry!" I blurted, hurtling into the library, and tossing my bag onto the nearest unsuspecting furniture. I raced toward the ladders. Dante, however, laid upside down on the red sofa with an assortment of colorful pillows, legs hooked over the edge while reading a book by the fire.

"Over here," he called, waving. "I found these for you." He sat up, revealing a small pile of books on the wooden coffee table. I made my way over, swallowing hard, thinking he had already dug through the shelves and those meager findings were all that turned up.

I sank into the yellow armchair, then read one of the titles. *Under the Light of the Italian Moon.*

What?

I picked up another. *A Day in India.* Another. *The Birth of Japan.*

"I find the chapters about nature and food to be the most fascinating. Though, the passages about fashion are also interesting. Oh," he handed me a polylingual dictionary. "And you shouldn't forget this unless you want to be molto perso."

I tilted my head at his words.

"'Very lost' in Italian," he clarified.

I gazed over the array of choices, each book representative of their respective countries. The vibrant teal of the Adriatic Sea. The luscious pink of cherry blossoms. The sandy yellow of the desert. "Dante, did you read all of these?"

He fiddled with his fingers. "No. Well, yes I suppose, if you mean I looked at the words and understood their meaning."

"That's what reading is."

He stood, ambling over to the bookshelves, hiding his face as he fiddled with his fingers. "It wasn't any problem. I had finished my homework anyway."

Even with Dante's speed, reading the six books I counted could not be accomplished in the hour I trained with Professor Norwood. Meaning, after I left his room, Dante completed his homework and read at least some of these books the night prior. I marveled at how he still stood when he received even less sleep than I did.

"Don't go trying to get rid of me this soon, Shyung," I teased, walking over to the heap of books we rudely left on the tables the night before. To be fair, it would be even more of a disaster attempting to put them all back.

He joined me, sitting down in a chair as he studied the mound. Nonchalantly, as if his lips bypassed the approval of his mind, he said, "I wouldn't want to."

His brain caught up with his words as his eyes widened in horror. Before he could notice, I sat down at the opposite side of the table, hiding my blushing cheeks behind the barrier of books.

———————— ∽◦❀◦∼ ————————

Dante and I tore through the books, checking the dates on each. Anything over one hundred years old was banished to the unuseful pile, leaving only a fraction of the books left. By the time we rooted out anything over a half-century old, only a handful remained.

"I don't get it," I said, looking between our new pile and the unuseful one. "Sightings of Mara occurred multiple times a year in countless countries until a half-century ago." I picked up the journal containing the French explorer's ghoulish drawing of Mara. "Then, they become less frequent. She's only ever spotted in and around France until twenty years ago where they stop completely. No trace of her at all."

"That must have been when she stopped to have a child, and then, a few years later, she gets exorcised." I hypothesized.

"Though it seems strange such a powerful demon would need to go on maternity leave."

"Wait…" Dante flipped between the five books we laid open, turning each to the intricate drawing or childish doodle the author provided. "Look." He pointed. The variations of Mara we grew accustomed to seeing no longer existed. All of the most recent depictions resembled each other in one way or another. A see-through figure. Shadows for eyes. A levitating body.

"She looks like a ghost, or a phantom, or…" I drew a hand to my mouth. "A poltergeist." One of the deadliest types of creatures, poltergeists differed from a standard campfire ghost. They didn't just moan and wander and maybe knock over a lamp if they were feeling real feisty. Poltergeists could *touch* the living. Scratching, biting, and clawing, wasn't even the worst of their habits. At their most vicious, poltergeists manipulated the elements. They were impossible to beat without the use of an exorcism spell. Aunt Esther had not taught me how to cast one, never seeing the need.

I grasped the arm of the chair closest to me, lowering myself down. My breath snagged in my chest and dread clutched my ribs, gripping each like the highest rung on a fifty-foot ladder.

"How… how am I ever going to beat *that*?"

"I…" Dante's mouth caught on his words, trying to think of a solution. "The Son of Mara… he's… well, he's been dormant for twenty years as far as we know. You have time to train."

"He was a baby for some of those years," I retorted.

"Maybe not. Some demons are born fully aged, especially powerful ones."

Sense and insanity fought for hold of my mind, leaving my body nauseous. They poisoned one another with their touch and I became unable to distinguish which was which.

"What if my powers don't accelerate in time?" I asked uneasily.

"The prophecy would disagree," Dante suggested.

My heart rolled its eyes at seeking solace in the so-called "divine" words of an ancient scroll. But logic weaseled its way through as images of the welling eyes and heart-struck smiles shrouded over the absurdity. Everyone else believed in the prophecy so deeply, so genuinely. Maybe I was the one who was mistaken.

"I suppose it would," I nodded, shedding the heavy skin of panic from my shoulders. "The prophecy says—or at the very least—*alludes* to me defeating him. Maybe not today, but a couple of tomorrows is all I need."

Dante placed his hand on mine, his grip as soothing.

"Or maybe like, several," I corrected.

MADISON MCMAHON

After we shelved our mess of books away, we perused over the countries of the world, finding comfort in dreaming up a life beyond now until the Bell welcomed us to dinner.

CHAPTER 17

After a night's rest, I managed to catch up on the classes I basically sleep walked through the day prior. More than that, I excelled in them. While the rest of my seasonal creaturology class used their allotted free time to chat (which I did not blame them for since we had only a period until lunch and hunger was already pecking away at me), I decided to read the following chapter of our textbook. Although I had a basic understanding from my homeschooling, this book was more up to date and in-depth about frost-biting fish, polarizing bears (rare and dangerous creatures that could pull your matter apart with a glance) and even griffapuffs. Foreboding knotted inside me the more I read. This recent edition said that if a griffapuff didn't find their pride in time, they would be picked off by the next one that found it. Aunt Esther never told me that, but maybe she wasn't aware.

Knowing my next class was mystical botany took my mind off the matter. Though I didn't do better in one subject over another, botany felt the most familiar. When we tended to the plants in the greenhouse, I slipped into the rhythm of nurturing the vegetables in the cottage garden, watering the flowers, listening to what they had to say. Though I detested the monotony of the life I knew just a week ago, it didn't hurt to feel the coolness of Aunt Esther's rings, guiding my hands as I dug, every once in a while.

As I made my way to class, my conversation with myself caused me to not realize there was no hum of voices coming from the greenhouse until it was too late.

"Good afternoon, Miss Seraphin," Headmaster Tenold nodded.

"Good afternoon, Headmaster," I replied. "What are you…"

He crossed his hands behind his back, straightening like the plants surrounding him, though, they were doing so apprehensively. "With the upcoming spectacle tomorrow, I figured having a little extra practice may be useful."

I clutched the straps of my bag. "But I have class right now," I laughed weakly.

"Oh, do not worry. Professor Honami has been made aware of your absence for today's lesson." Under the glass panels of the room, the Headmaster appeared almost translucent.

Something crept from my stomach and hovered heavily in my chest. If the Headmaster of the school was suggesting I miss one class, then it must be for the greater good. He was right. He was the Headmaster. I dismissed the feeling arising in me as nothing more than an impatient appetite.

"I didn't know Professor Norwood has this period free," I said, setting my bag down beside a potted venus fly trap standing at my height.

"Professor Norwood will not be joining us. As you are progressing so quickly, I thought we might…" He adjusted his circular glasses. "Broaden your training."

With that, a puff of smoke arose from the corner of the room. Swatting away the stench of whatever he did, Sigmis Bayle sauntered out from behind the plants. His grin dripped with ostentation as if it was sweat.

"Mr. Bayle will be your sparring partner for today," The Headmaster announced.

My face went slack. "*Sparring?*"

"I can assure you, Miss Seraphin, Mr. Bayle has had plenty of practice training with his father. He is aware that you both are not battling to harm but to come to a checkmate. Once you corner your opponent, you win. If anything should go astray, I will stop the match."

"I—I, um, sir—" I sputtered. My thoughts halted, intertwined, entangled themselves as they tried to formulate into words why this was not something I wanted to do. I still had more time before… before.

"No need to cause yourself wrinkles," Bayle said smugly. "I couldn't live with myself if I scorched your pretty face."

This was the first time we had spoken since he...

I shivered the memory away, digging my nails into my palm to keep the memory from personifying.

He wanted to do this? Fine. I had more than enough indignation to draw from to sweep his pride into the realms of the past.

"Gentlemen first," I said, joining him at the open center of the room. "Though, that first part doesn't apply to you very much, so I suppose it's just *men first*." I eyed him up and down. His ridiculous grey silk shirt and pants—no, as a matter of fact, his whole wardrobe could not compare to the one suit Gus wore. Even with his small stature, Gus bore his attire with dignity while Bayle merely wished to strut. "Well... boy," I corrected myself.

He tried to suppress the agitation I had caused him, but I caught it quick enough to swipe it behind his knees, causing him to land on his back. He huffed back to his feet. Without wasting another breath, he charged right for me. I snatched up his determination and aimed it towards him, but he jumped to my right. Igniting only the tip of his finger, he rolled past me, dragging the spark across the hem of my dress. The flame slithered up, and I frantically patted it out. Before I could process the bite taken out of one of my only clothes, Bayle appeared at the right side of the room, lurking behind a row of carnivorous trees.

He shot his hand forward but not at me. A burst of fire knocked

the trees over one by one, catching them alight as the flames

dripped from one to another. I jumped out of the way before a

branch could concuss and consume me with fire.

"Headmaster!" I called back to him in the corner he

stood in. "Stop the match! All the plants will die!"

He remained silently observant. The Bell rang for lunch.

I whipped around. The fire was as greedy as its maker.

It had searched out the smallest opening to devour the other

plants. As it trickled towards the other tables, I noticed the labels

on each pot. *Jiménez.* A few more down. *Chaumont.* Another.

Charlie. The tallest of the seedlings belonged to *Shyung.* As the

Headmaster stood silently, I feared he would remain the same if

accusations arose, blaming the student who caused it in *Tenold's*

sparring match.

"I said stop!" I thrust both of my hands out towards the

line of destruction. Water from the watering cans surged out of the

funnel, sniping the flames instantly. I heaved as smoke twirled

from the blackened corpses of the trees. My stomach felt as if

someone was hollowing it out and starting to carve into my chest.

Manipulating water was new. Manipulating so much of it was

apparently exhausting.

Across the room, I watched Bayle's go alight with understanding. He let his grin unravel slowly, playing with the flame balling in his hand. He hurled it towards the left side of the room where the flowers could only recoil back so far before their roots forced them to accept their fate. I cast my hands out again.

There was no more water in the cans.

Before I could think of a second move, Bayle clapped his hands together, charring whatever poor soul he had ripped from life, and blew the ash in my face. It blasted up my nose, and stung my eyes. I fell to my hands and knees, coughing and heaving. Snot and tears pooled in my nose and eyes, attempting to flush out what felt like bees that bite.

"Stop," The Headmaster said in his monotone voice. "Mr. Bayle, please find Miss Aquis. She will extinguish the flames." Through my blurred vision, I saw Bayle wink at me before departing. My heart twisted in on itself, thick with dread. Now standing above me, the Headmaster handed me a handkerchief. I wondered if his rigid posture prevented him from bending down or if he simply refused to bring himself to a lower level.

I blotted my eyes and blew my nose, but they still stung raw.

"Your main objective is to defeat your opponent," he said placidly. "You can not be so concerned with your surroundings when battling."

I looked up at him, the sunlight causing my eyes to pluck with tears again. "What if those plants were people? The prophecy says I will save all, not just myself," I rasped.

"Miss Seraphin, please. Consider the greater good. If your enemy defeats you first, the people remaining will fall."

"But if—" I clutched my chest as my words tumbled into a fit of hacking. Each cough scraped my insides from my chest to my throat. I breathed in the sharp scent of burning leaves, and my stomach swelled with the unbearable weight of nothing.

"Once Mr. Bayle returns, he can escort you to the infirmary—"

"No," I grated out. "I can manage myself."

"Very well." The Headmaster nodded, departing without even a glance at the corpses of trees or the blazes set to the flowers, swallowing any color or life they possessed.

Reaching to the table above me, I pulled myself up. Buoyant blood pooled into my eyes and my vision became spotted with dots so white they went blue. I steadied my body against the row of death before me, forcing myself to breath

In. Out.

Innnn. Outttt.

Innnnnnnnn. Outttttttttt.

The darkness drew back and my vision restored to a low blur. I leaned against the tables and I put out a foot to walk. My mind toppled over before my body did. The adrenaline of the fight pushed away the plaguing exhaustion.

The Bell rang, signaling the end of lunch. My stomach bounded up through my ribs, grating against my lungs, and I puked up the anxiety of it all.

"Bly!" A voice exclaimed. A flurry of yellow, black, and more black raced towards me. Sidestepping the puddle of vomit, Clyde, Dante, and Gus bent down at my side. "You weren't at lunch so we went looking for you..." Clyde looked between the puke and my leaking face. "Are you sick?"

"I don't think she can vomit fire," Gus said, surveying the destruction.

Dante placed a hand on my shoulder, his concern forcing me to meet his eyes, or what I could make of them. "Did someone attack you?"

"I..." I choked on my words, coughing. Clyde brought a plate of food into my vision. I immediately went for the soup. Thankfully, it had gone cold because I gulped it down, attempting to coat my throat. As I lowered the bowl from my face, Clyde used her sleeve to wipe my eyes, nose, and mouth. The fuzz of my brain cleared away and I became slightly embarrassed of the sick all over the floor.

"Blythe?" Dante asked again. The three of them stared at me, Clyde concerned, Gus bothered, and Dante, both.

"Tenold pulled me out of class for training." I stopped to let out the cough building, less harsh than before, thankfully. "He brought Bayle to duel with me."

"Duel?" Dante recoiled back, an anger bubbling in him.

"It was practice for when…" I let them finish my thought.

"Sigmis did this?" Clyde asked. Her face delved into a layer of worry I had never once seen a remote hint of. It horrified me to be the cause of it.

Dante's forehead wrinkled as his eyes became a midnight storm. "Tenold allowed him to do this to you?"

"It…" I let out the cough tickling my throat. "He was just trying to prepare me and now, I can see he was right to do so."

"She can't be serious," Gus retorted.

"I am." I shot back. "I couldn't defeat Bayle, so how am I going to defeat the Son of Mara? I just…" I stifled a cough in fear of undoing the soup's healing effects. "I'll just train harder."

"Bly…" Clyde wiped my nose.

"It's okay, really. I'll be fine." I mustered a smile. Wherever Bayle was, it didn't matter anymore because the fires had withered out. Their victim's remains were finally able to bury themselves in their soil. Their home. Though the scent of charred wood and burnt petals would reappear whenever I looked at their replacements, I was soothed by the untouched potted projects in the corner. "All this and more would be worth it just to be here with you all." They appreciated my sentiments, but exchanged troubled glances with one another. Their concern was valid, maybe even right, but I couldn't afford to give into that cycle of mistrust. It would only bring homesickness, and I had to prove I could live outside of the cottage. I had to trust the person in charge of doing the one thing my aunt asked of me—to hone my power. More than that, I had to trust the person guiding me through the prophecy. I had to believe there was a good reason for it all.

CHAPTER 18

The amber sunlight nudged my eyes open. I stretched out my joints, soaking in the strange absence of... noise.

I looked over at Melsella's bed where she still laid fast asleep under a mound of lush covers. My throat itched a little as I giggled, but I couldn't help it at the surprising turn of events. Instead of hounding her—as she would have done to me—, I chose to offer a kind pat on the shoulder to wake her.

"Melsella..." I whispered delicately. "It's time for cl—"

Suddenly, she sucked in a violent gasp as if returning from the dead. She ripped off her gray satin night mask, eyes swollen with sleep and aggravation.

"Gods below, Blythe! What are you doing?"

"We have to get ready for class," I reminded her, gesturing to the morning light streaming through the window.

Melsella groaned, flopping back down on the bed, making her plush pillows bounce.

"Classes are cancelled today," she looked at me sharply before pulling her mask back over her eyes and rolling over.

"What? Why?"

"Your ceremony," she mumbled through her drowsiness.

"Ceremony? No, the Headmaster said it was just a spectacle. A show for the students," I clarified.

"Really? Then why did he invite the newspapers?"

Newspapers? Between this week and last, I was getting whiplash. Last week nobody knew me except for my aunt and maybe the vendor who always let me take an extra sample. Now newspapers (plural) were coming to see me? They would write and print pictures of *me*?

A knock interrupted my thoughts.

Melsella bolted out of bed, yelling: "Wait! Wait!" She flew over to her chest, shimmied out of her nightgown, and wrangled herself into a dress. Once she situated herself into a silver dress with puffed sleeves, I opened the door. It was too early to care if someone saw my plain nightgown anyways. It's not like I had a fashion reputation to uphold.

On the other side stood Headmaster Tenold. His usual white coat and dress shoes reflected the lights of the candles in the hall, but his ordinarily erratic hair was combed neatly down, making the years stress had taken from him look a little less in number.

"Good morning, Miss Seraphin." He nodded to me, then acknowledging my roommate frantically brushing her hair, "Miss Melsella."

He stood with his hands behind his back and a faint smile pasted on his mouth. In my short time at Esalroth, the Headmaster never curled his mouth unless pronouncing a word that required so. "I hope you are well for you have a rather important day ahead of you. You see, I took the liberty of—"

"I already told her!" Melsella raised her hand, smiling proudly.

Slightly irritated, the Headmaster continued, "Ah, well, then I suppose I only have this for you then." He extended his hand to a golden dining cart sitting in the hallway. He wheeled it inside, and the yolks of plump eggs jiggled, and fresh orange juice swirled in its glass. The dew of fresh fruits in bowls and butter of toast on plates shined in the morning sun. With Chucks, I could ask for any breakfast I wanted, but I had never dreamed so big. Porridge, oatmeal, and the occasional fruit pancake were all I had grown accustomed to eating for breakfast. Though unease crept up my spine at the more than generous gesture, I brushed it away.

It was just a kind thing to do.

"Thank you, Headmaster," I replied, eyes fixed on the heavenly assortment. The Headmaster bowed his head in reply. "Eat all the strength you can, Miss Seraphin. I will be back to walk you to the ceremony ten minutes before noon." He started to leave but pointed his finger upward with an *ah* as if remembering something. "Also, your father sent you a letter. I left it on the cart. You can give your response to me in my office and I will mail it to him."

I blinked at him, confusion rattling my brain.

My father had never sent me a letter.

"O-okay, thanks."

The Headmaster nodded and left, his brown leather shoes matching the dark wood of the floor.

"You, um…" I stumbled over my words while reaching for the crisp white letter propped up on a bowl of blueberries. "You can have some of this, Melsella."

Melsella scurried over, plucking a strawberry from a bowl. "Ooo, these must be freshly picked! They're still wet."

Melsella's ravings about the farms on Mount Olympus went fuzzy as I took in the envelope.

Blythe Seraphin was scrawled across it in my father's childish handwriting.

Creasing it with my tightening grip, I tried to guess at the contents. Was he asking how I liked school? Who I had met? What I had learned?

Apologizing for not writing so soon?

THE SON OF MARA

No. If this letter contained so much as a "sorry", I would know it was a fake. My father was nothing if not always right.

I slipped my fingernail under the seal and opened the flap. I pulled out a tea stained page half the size of a normal paper. Including hellos and goodbyes, which left only enough room for an inquiry or two. Not nearly enough space to rave about one's daughter. I scolded myself for thinking the foolish idea that now stung worse than yesterday. Hasty penmanship slanted across the page. The strokes pressed so hard into the paper the backside had reverse indents of the writing. I startled at how, despite not even reading a word, the letter looked almost… angry.

My grumbling stomach compelled me to read it before the savory scents of my delivered breakfast drove me mad.

Blythe,

Your Aunt Esther has informed me you are now attending Esalroth Academy. I am sure you are the one who convinced her of such an outlandish idea. This goes against my very clear instruction that you are not to attend school—no matter the circumstance. How could you leave your aunt by herself? We will discuss your behavior and… accident when I return, but as of now, you will leave Esalroth and return home. To confirm this, please mail a copy of your withdrawal papers to the address below. I understand postal travel takes time without the medical urgency stamp I am provided, so I expect your letter to arrive no later than the third week of October. If you fail to do so, I will

come there and bring you home myself.

Think of your aunt, Blythe.

-Adam Seraphin, your father

The address given came from India.

After years of silence, my father took a break from curing those on the brink of death to tell me I could not attend school. After Aunt Esther teaching me shapes. After Aunt Esther showing me how to write. After Aunt Esther just being there he thought he now had a say in raising me?

My father was a man of tradition. Did children not go to school?

I let out a laugh. A dry. Mocking. Laugh.

"Did someone write a good joke?" Melsella asked, finishing the last of the strawberries and plopping the stems into an empty bowl.

"Yeah," I replied. "Yeah, they did." I flopped down on my bed, letting the aggression trickle down my back and down to the deepest circles of hell.

I tossed the letter aside, letting it slip between the side of my bed and the wall.

Adam Seraphin, your father.

Of course, the Adam Seraphin came before his familial status.

Melsella and I regretted gorging on the buffet as we had to relinquish the rest of our time to laying on our beds, grumbling about how full we were.

After what felt like hours, I managed to wriggle into my favorite outfit—a light copper dress with a skirt I could twirl in. It was the closest and most affordable version I could get of my favorite color—the deepest red you could mix together. A shade of great emotions. Love, rage, lust, hate. My spirit swirled just imagining the fabric against my strawberry-blonde hair braided in a bun. It leaped at the idea of asking Clyde to fashion me such a dress for the ball. Though, I contained the thought to only a dream as I knew Clyde was busy sewing her own. Maybe next year.

While my stomach deflated, I read the books Dante took out for me. I started with Italy as that was the closest of all the countries. As I finished reading about Milan—noting to tell Clyde there was a fashion capital of the whole *world*—another knock sounded at the door. The same one-two pattern as before. The Headmaster.

I gave myself another once over in Melsella's mirror, combing down any flyaways with my fingers. With the combination of my copper dress, grey eyes, and strawberry blonde hair, Aunt Esther claimed I looked like a magical root from the river used for love potions.

I slipped into my boots, hopping on one leg to the door as I did so. Using the floor, I jammed my foot into my right shoe as I opened the door. The Headmaster stood as upright as he did hours before and not a hair left askew by the day's work.

"Hello, Miss Seraphin. Are—" He looked down, assessing my attire. "Is this what you will be wearing to the ceremony?"

Heat crossed my cheeks, but I tried to remain unphased. "Yes."

He took in my words, contemplating the proper way to state the dissatisfaction I sensed in him. He looked to Melsella who's satin dress commanded the sun to trace its pleated skirt.

"Miss Melsella, would you be so generous as to lend Miss Seraphin some more... formal attire."

I looked at the Headmaster, brows fluctuating between furrowing themselves or raising. "Sir?"

Thin wisps of the Headmaster's hair seemed to stick upright as if this conversation was frazzling him. "Please pardon my intrusion. I am only protecting you from the childish scrutiny of the press. They all have different expectations of who the one will appear to be, so it's best to stick with a safer option. Like, say...," He looked at Melsella. "Something in white?"

Melsella chirped in excitement, rummaging through her chest. From about half-way down, she pulled out a dress the color of a pearl. Ruffles circled the hips and reappeared again at the ankle length bottom. The thought of wearing such a clean dress tantalized my nerves with anxiety. Not only did I not own white clothes because the color bored me, but wearing such a pristine dress at home would be a sure way to get it dirty.

You're not at home anymore, Blythe, I chided myself. I would have died for such tailoring at home.

Melsella rushed over to me, laying the dress against my body. I could only imagine how I looked. A witch pretending to be an angel.

"Perfect!" Melsella declared.

Perfect, I told myself.

"Please join me in the hall after you dress," The Headmaster instructed, placing his hand on the door knob, but before he shut it, he poked his head back in. "Oh, and try to cover those shoes as best you can."

Tenold closed the door, and I stared down at my boots, forever speckled with aged mud. I realized I had never given much thought to my appearance, if I was even pretty. No one saw me but my aunt and myself, and Aunt Esther certainly never said I was ugly. But, I had never grown up knowing exactly what pretty was. What it looked like. Acted like.

I guess it was another new thing to learn.

MADISON MCMAHON

CHAPTER 19

The Headmaster had to open the door to the outside carefully in order to not hit the students, reporters, and strange mechanical boxes on stilts packed into the courtyard.

As we said excused ourselves through the crowd, their rampant chatter fell like dominos into hushed whispers.

Look! It's time.

She's right over there!

She's here.

The people behind the mechanical boxes snatched them up and pointed them towards me. A bright light flashed from them, and I jumped back, covering my eyes so they wouldn't blind me.

"That's only a camera, Miss Seraphin," The Headmaster whispered to me, and I gave him a puzzled look in return. "They capture images of real life and put them on paper to be seen."

I marveled at the idea.

See, I told myself. *You never would have known such a thing if you had not come here. If the Headmaster hadn't invited you here.*

The crowd parted for us without me even needing to utter an excuse me, like my presence alone was able to be sensed. Right where the courtyard became the woods, a makeshift stage waited with a table stacked with parchment on top. I crossed onto the stage, hiking my dress up to not trip on its length, as the words on the papers became legible: Worry no longer, the one has come to vanquish your fears.

Right on time, the clock overlooking the courtyard struck noon.

"Ladies, gentleman, and other kind folks," The Headmaster addressed the crowd, his voice silencing them with the first syllable. "Thank you for joining us today to witness history. We all have waited very long for this moment, but now it has finally arrived. A young witch unaided by an herb, card, or element." The crowd gasped. "Miss Blythe Seraphin has finally come." Headmaster Tenold extended his arm towards me, and the crowd burst into cheers. The camera's lamps exploded into white light, and I waved to everyone, hoping that was what the one was supposed to do.

My heart thumped in my ears as the Headmaster whispered, "Start with something small and then dispense the papers over them." With that, he stepped back behind the table, holding his arms in front of him at the wrist.

I approached the table as if it would bite, feeling the weight of hundreds of antsy limbs and hungry eyes. My dress stuck to my body as a hot chill waved over me. This is what you wanted, I reminded myself. You wanted to be noticed.

But by this many people I didn't even know?

I tuned into my spirit for guidance, who never once had lied to me. It put its ear to my chest, feeling the restless anticipation of the crowd like a herd of ants crawling across skin. But underneath that thin layer something pulsated. Something that used the ants as a decoy to drive this other feeling—hope.

I took a single piece of paper in my hands and laid it across the table. I could feel the crowd inching forward, trying to get a glimpse. I folded down the top corners, then the entire page in half. Finally, I creased both sides and held up my creation. A paper airplane.

I walked to the front of the stage, hunching slightly to not let my dirty boots peek out from under my dress, and placed it down on the floor. At my every movement, the pulsation from the crowd pounded quicker, more intensely. Rubbing the sensation between my index finger and thumb, I gave the air a flick, and the paper airplane soared over the crowd. It rocketed upwards, then spiraled back down in a loose curl so no matter where you stood, everyone could witness the self-flying creation. Gasps propelled it forward, and their pulses burst into pure awe. All movement ceased, as if blinking was secondary to witnessing this event. I piloted it just inches over the crowd, letting it circle around until a pure white hand snatched it. Yellow eyes beamed with glee.

"Scrapbook moment!" Clyde exclaimed, standing on the bench next to Dante and Gus, who huddled into themselves, but couldn't help laughing. "Way to go, Bly!!"

I allowed myself a laugh before returning back to the table. There appeared to be fifty or more pages stacked finely on top of one another—more anythings than I'd ever used my power on before.

My spirit sensed my dismay and returned the favor of finally paying it attention. It took hold of my lungs, forcing them to breathe. Then it scrambled to my brain, wrenching away the clouds muddling my thoughts. As it gave me the thumbs up, I stilled my body. Exhilaration curled through the crowd, buzzing into my fingertips and through to my shoulders. I put both of my hands forward and gave a firm swish as if conducting a one-note symphony. The papers trailed one another into the air, forming a literary staircase. As the last page joined, I twirled the pieces in a circle, giving the courtyard an ivory halo.

Looking out onto the crowd's astonished faces, punctuated by the occasional flashes of light, I wished my aunt's hazel eyes were among them. I wish she could see me here, honing my power, preparing to defeat an *evil demon*. If that wasn't good, I don't know what was. Not only would her olive face glow with pride, but freedom.

She would be free. She could *live*.

We could live.

I spun the papers around with a flourish, only heightening the spark of the crowd. But while the papers revolved overheard, the exhilaration became threaded with another feeling—spite. My smile rose as I tried to imagine my father when I wasn't making papers fly, but defeating a demon. *The* Son of Mara.

The rationale of the letter fell into place. He must have known of the prophecy. My father, the *great good of the earth*, would not be the most notable Seraphin.

I would be.

I went to think of my father's envious face but found the only version I could recall was the stoic portrait I used to pass every day on the living room mantle.

Good.

As I gazed up at the ring of parchment, a thump sounded from the clock. The panel between the six and seven strokes opened on its hinges. The possibility that a screw had gone loose dissipated when fire snaked upwards towards the papers, pricking each one. Their ends started to curl brown. I let go of my grip on the pages while fear curdled in my stomach. The black exterior of the clock made it too dark to see who was inside, but *someone* had to be in there. I had only just learned what a camera was, but I was certain clocks did not breathe fire.

"Blythe," A firm hand gripped my shoulder. Professor Norwood's. I had not heard her climb the steps in my panic. "Stop this." Her voice wobbled, fright creeping into its chords. "Please."

"Isadore," Headmaster Tenold stepped in. "Let her show the people what she can do."

"This is not my doing," I replied. Then, suddenly, a single, untouched paper broke from the ashes of its siblings and drifted to my feet. Flames sparked on the page and began to carve a singular word.

STOP

I jolted back, the eager eyes of the crowd puzzled as to why I was scared of my own trick. The realization rushed through my veins, frigid and relentless. Not one person at Esalroth so much as suggested I ignore the prophecy, let alone stop what I was doing. Everyone treated me as though I was a necessity to ensure their livelihood. The one, singular soulless being that would fall at my existence lived in the same prophecy as I.

The Son of Mara.

But he was not just *at* Esalroth.

THE SON OF MARA

Instead of attacking from above, hidden in back of the tall spires, or from the sides, ducked behind the bushes or trees—all easier options—he struck from the clock.

A fever's sweat palmed my forehead, transfiguring my body until the only thing I knew, the only thing I had ever felt, was cold heat.

It was not ordinary for such large clocks to open outward.

To know the clock's opening meant the Son of Mara was a student.

CHAPTER 20

Led by Professor Norwood, the teachers herded the confused students back to their rooms while the Headmaster thanked the reporters for their presence, explaining the event had to be cut short due to a mechanical error.

Out of all the depictions of Mara, I had never seen 'mechanical error' as one of them.

My head spun as Professor Norwood took me by the arm and brought me to my room. I wriggled free from her grip when we got to my door. "Professor, the Son—" I started.

"Miss Seraphin," The effort it took for her to maintain the usual evenness in her voice made me reel. She knew I was right. "Please stay in your room until further notice."

"But—"

She held up a firm hand, the delicate silver color of her thin pinky ring shining in the flickering lights of the hall as if they were sounding a silent alarm. "The faculty will search and secure the school. Please stay in your room until further notice." The Professor turned, her cape moving fiercely behind her.

"I can help! That's what I'm *supposed* to do!" I called back. Doubt crept into my afterthought. The certainty I believed, that I clung to so hopefully, had crumbled. I no longer had time. If I found the Son of Mara right now, would I be able to defeat him?

Yes, I reminded myself. *The prophecy says so.*

Yesterday would say otherwise.

The Professor looked at me with her eyes the color of well-loved leather books. She placed both hands on my shoulder. I expected to feel comfort rippling through her palms, but a twinge of grief pricked me.

"I would never forgive myself if I had to tell Esther something had... gone wrong." As I took into account how she cradled my aunt's name like she feared it would slip away, I noticed she was rolling her thumb over the ring on her pinky. An absent-minded habit that would mean nothing if I did not feel another twinge from her pinch me. Not just slip away. Slip away *again.*

Professor Norwood hardened. "Please stay in your room until further notice."

I let her march down the hall while I stayed planted, dealing with the fact the lights had come up on the villain in my story and would never turn off again.

I knocked on my door, more annoyed than ever that I still had not received a way into my own room. I battered away at my thoughts while pounding on the door. Finally, after long enough of knocking that my knuckles were sore, the door opened to reveal Melsella's head as if she turned the knob and pivoted away as quickly as she could.

Not as if. She did.

She went back to her desk, hovering intensely over an assignment.

"Melsella?" I asked, unnerved by the absence of her energy and even more so that I was disturbed by its loss. "Are you okay?"

She remained silent, writing more vehemently.

"The teachers will find the Son of Mara and I'll go and I'll… I'll defeat him," I assured her, despite having just pulled the plan out of thin air.

The beginning of fall wind rustled against the window.

"I promise I'm not going to let anything happen," I hoped, putting my hand on her shoulder. "It's okay—"

"I don't need your protection, Blythe! I am part *god*," She spat, pushing up from the chair.

"What's your problem?" I shot back.

She looked utterly assaulted. "My problem? Do you know why there are so few mythical people in this hall? Why would we bother attending a school that doesn't reside in a place like Olympus? We were *invited* here by Tenold for the same reason as you."

I stared at her, taken aback.

"Honestly, I thought you were no different. Just another grasp at smoke. I believed the reporters and ceremony were a bit dramatic compared to the feast held for me when I arrived here at twelve." The mockery in her voice gave way to honest pain. "Do you know how disappointed my family was when the belief I was anything special fizzled out? The belief I wasn't just some defect who couldn't even fly without these wings?" She pointed to her feet, the wings strapped to them tucked around her ankles.

"You can manipulate the wind," I rebutted. "That *is* special."

"Oh, but not like you. You're so the chosen one you brought the Son of Mara to Esalroth."

"Do you hear yourself?" I narrowed my eyes at her, stepping closer. "An actual demon is roaming our school, and all you can think of is yourself. Why am I even surprised by that?" I threw my hands down. "That's all you have *ever* thought about." I pointed at her.

She crossed her arms. "I offered to share a room with you because I know what it's like to feel you're an outsider even though everyone knows who you are. *What* you are. That is not selfish."

"Awesome, but do you know what is? How you treat Dante, and Gus, and Charlie. They feel like outsiders too, but they're not the palatable kind of loner, are they? They come from places you've only heard stories, *rumors*, about. Instead of asking them about it, or I don't know, simply being kind to them, you believe those lies for your own self-preservation. To keep the world as you know it. A hero and a monster. A god and a villain."

Melsella frowned, lowering her voice. "Stories read that way for a reason. It's just... easier."

"You didn't do the easy thing when you picked to be my roommate, or chose to stay at Esalroth even though you're not the one. Why pick the easy way now?" I turned away from her. "Look, I am not going to speak on their behalf," I pulled her dress over my head, careful to not tear it in my anger. "But I'm not going to stand here while you wallow." I grabbed my copper dress that I threw hastily on the bed and put it on. It was slightly wrinkled, but it was *mine*. I made for the door, feeling Melsella heavy gaze on me.

"Where are you going?" She called.

"To save you all."

CHAPTER 21

I clung to the hallway walls, peaking around the corner. *The teachers must have already secured the dorms.* Even so, I kept my footwork light as I crept down the monstrous hall. The faded chatter from students studying or gossiping together had been sucked from the air, leaving each step of my boot eerily loud. The lights continued to flicker with warning as I tapped quietly on room 66,599.

"Dante?" I whispered. "It's Blythe."

Dante's face appeared through the crack, and I slipped inside. The simple neatness of his room was upended. Books laid scattered on the floor, some open as if they had been violently read through. His trunk was toppled over, the contents of it spewed throughout the room. Looking down at my feet, I recognized his one blanket was flung from his bed that now had been ripped bare, leaving everything down to his sheets strewn across the exposed mattress.

166

"What happened?" I asked. The barest hint of a frown hung from his lips.

"They wanted to make sure no one helped the Son of Mara get in," he replied, looking over his mangled room.

"Dante," I looked at him, but he couldn't pry his eyes away. "The Son of Mara is a student here."

"What?" He swiveled his head towards me. "How do you know?"

"Why go through the trouble of breaking into the school when you can just attack from above or the sides? And then there's the question of how he would know the clock opened outwards."

Realization struck Dante. He ran a hand through his thick hair that looked like it had been searched through as well. "So he has been shapeshifting all this time?"

"That's what I thought at first too, but Esalroth doesn't have that many students," I replied. "It would be easily noticed if someone was shapeshifting, pretending to be multiple students." Dante's eyes darted around the room in thought.

"Basic magical genetics tells us that magical children don't inherit all their parents' powers unless their parents are the same species. Like if a vampire and a fire nymph had a child, that child might have fangs but not be afflicted by the sun. It might have the ability to manipulate fire but not create it." I said, starting to pick up his books and returning them back to their place beside his bed. He followed suit with his trunk, keeping his anxious body at work while our minds spun. "Depending on who she had the child with, her son must only have a limited variety of her powers."

"So, either he can't shapeshift, or he's been smart enough to stick to one form," Dante added while refolding his clothes.

"Exactly," I replied. Eyes alight, I made my way to the door. "We need to go tell Tenold."

"No," Dante jumped up. "We can't. He'll only do more of..." He surveyed his room that was just starting to look halfway decent again. "This."

Dante was right. Any monstrous student would have their room capsized over and over until the Headmaster found an answer that satisfied him.

"Then, we'll narrow it down ourselves," I decided. "If you want to, I mean."

"Yes," he replied immediately. "However, Esalroth isn't in any short supply of students without a parent or two," he stated.

"You're right," I replied. "We'll have to work our way around, and I know just who to start with. Someone I was glad was missing from the ceremony at first."

Dante furrowed his brows. "Who?"

MADISON MCMAHON
"Son of the god of *fire* and wielding, Sigmis Bayle."

———————————⟋∘⊗∘⟍———————————

Dante and I sucked in our breaths until we practically became part of the wall. Dante's high-necked black tunic walking across the light blue carpet may very well have been the equivalent of the night deciding it wanted to exist during the daytime.

I checked the markings of each door in the mythical hall. Across the hall from my room and two doors down, I spotted a flame engraved on the door in gold.

Found it.

I raised my hand to the door, bracing myself to knock. What if we were right? What if Bayle was the Son of Mara, and we were walking right into his very room?

Wide eyes and ancient parchment blurred across my mind.

Miss Seraphin has finally come.

I was destined to defeat the Son of Mara. The Headmaster said so.

I rapped on the door as quietly as possible. A moment later, a profoundly sun-tanned face buttoned with brown eyes answered. A lazy grin emerged. I bit down on my tongue to keep the bile from rising in my throat.

"What do we have here?" He asked, eyeing me, then less favorably, Dante.

"We need to talk. Will you let us in, please?" I displayed the polite attitude I knew he would absorb like a blonde succubus.

"Come on in," he smiled, extending his arm inside.

I expected nothing less from the bedroom of Bayle. The room feigned an impression of a rich welder's room. Heavy pieces of metal showered the area in bulky decor. A mirror. A shield. A hammer. An anvil. Anything that Bayle could pretend he earned. In its center rested a bed with a silver frame, carved to appear as though on fire.

"I am awfully sorry about our duel the other day," he pretended to pout, his eyes wild with desire. "Though, it means we will have to practice again."

Dante stiffened beside me, fists clenching.

"Where were you during the ceremony?" I asked.

Bayle gave an amused laugh. "Did you miss me?"

I stifled my scowl despite my spirit scratching my insides to pounce on him.

Keep pretending.

"I only wish you invited me to wherever you went," I sauntered around the room, taking in his overcompensating decor.

"You wouldn't have liked it much, sweetheart," he grinned, leisurely bearing his teeth like a lion stalking its prey. I couldn't help but cringe.

"I don't know about Blythe, but I sure have a fear of heights," Dante intercepted, eyes growing dark.

"What?" Bayle squinted at him, annoyed.

"The clock is almost two stories up. Did you take a sedative to stay calm? I need to know for when *I* go attack another student."

I shot Dante a warning look. If my guess was correct, I didn't want him taking the brunt of the Son of Mara's fury.

"Is that what this is about?" Bayle's eyes boiled with anger while he looked between us. As his gaze fixed on me, he let out a chuckle—a low, derisive gurgle from the pit of the stomach. "If I were going to attack you," He stepped closer to me with intentional delay as if he wanted to savor every moment he got to look at me while having the upper hand. I prepared myself, already feeling around for emotion to draw from. Dante's temper, fighting to stay caged. Bayle's bubbling amusement.

"If I were going to attack you," he repeated. My breath caught. He was too close. Too, too, too close. "I wouldn't have left you eyes to see my little note."

Crossing the distance between them in two strides, Dante grabbed Bayle by the collar of his ash-colored suit. His knuckles

whitened as he came so close to Bayle's face he could have
pricked him with a fang.

"Where. Were. You," Dante fumed. Bayle tensed under his
grip, understanding fighting would be a mistake.

"I wasn't in the clock tower," he hissed. "I was here. I
didn't want to watch your stupid *play*. You know," he scoffed. "I
would have still believed I was the one if you didn't drag the Son
of Mara out from the pits of hell," he snarled at me.

I placed a hand on Dante's shoulder. "We're done here."
From Bayle's brazen attitude to how he held under Dante's grasp,
if Bayle was the Son of Mara he would not be postponing a fight.

Dante toughened his grip on Bayle, eyes darkening,
searching.

"Dante," I pressed again. "It's not him."

He warned Bayle once more with the boundless shadows
of his eyes before releasing him and storming out the door,
leaving a trail of fizzling wrath.

CHAPTER 22

"Dante!" I whispered a shout. He continued down the hall with his hands by his side. Something that had been fermenting for too long steamed off of him. He turned back down the monstrous hall as I trotted after him.

He didn't shut the door completely when he entered his room, acquiescing I was bound to follow.

I entered slowly, finding Dante sitting on his disheveled bed with his hands on his knees.

"What happened there?" I asked.

"He threatened you," he said, eyes fixed on the floor boards.

"That's not what I meant," I returned. "Your reaction seemed far more personal than taunts with no backing."

His shoulders deflated as he clasped his hands together, methodically tracing his knuckles. "I used to have a family in Taiwan. A mom and a dad. An older and younger sister. And we lived on a farm." I could see him steadying himself with every reminiscence. "When I was eight, I had a nightmare of a spindly woman the size of our home. One by one, she sucked our animals' blood bone dry. Then, she turned to me with eyes like a molten abyss and hissed with this raspy voice, '*your turn*'."

He took a hollow breath. "I woke up screaming. I was running out of the house before I could even process where I was going. I just ran. Through the fields. Through the trees, until I ran into a stack of cold flesh. It grinned at me with these teeth the size of talons. He bit me, and I shrieked. I shrieked so loud my family found me. The vampire whisked away before it could kill me, but before I could even feel it, as soon as I looked into my family's eyes and saw the fear taking root, I knew I was transformed."

I swallowed hard.

"And so, I ran. I ran until I found a city. I ran for years until I couldn't stomach I had become just like the monster who ruined my life. And not the vampire who bit me. *Mara*."

Realization settled like a boulder in my chest. "Some cultures believe she's the reason children have nightmares," I recited.

He looked up at me, eyes as set as midnight. "I'm not running anymore."

A memory that didn't fit quite right tumbled out. "Is that why you stopped me the first day we met? When I went to run out of the library?"

"That humid panic that makes the world seem to morph in height and width—that was the last thing I ever truly felt." The lump in his throat bobbed up and down.

"Dante, I'm—" Sorry. The silencing word my aunt would repeat to me whenever I asked of my mother. She was *sorry*, but that was for my father to talk to me about. Each time she repeated it, it felt like a slice at my pain. Like a five letter word was supposed to equivocate to over a decade of confusion, anger, and loss. "We're going to find him. We're going to end this."

He nodded. "Thanks."

"No problem," I nudged his shoulder. "I have a way with words." He laughed, and it was like clouds had tumbled out over the beating sun of a summer's day, enveloping you in the shade. "But how can I help you as of now?"

He shook his head as he stood, giving a brittle laugh. "You can't go back to the past."

I looked at him. "Try me."

He considered me for a moment before letting his desire dislodge itself from the tomb of where he allowed himself to dream. "I wish I could have been a kid."

THE SON OF MARA

His request was so simple, something that should have been a guarantee. While I did not possess the power of time travel, I did have the knowledge of a lonely girl who had learned to entertain herself. Pulling the sheets left askew on his bed, I lifted one side overhead, using the pushpin from one of his paintings to tack it in place. Using another pin, I tacked the other side to the corner his bed was tucked in. While it looked more like a tent cut in half, I beamed at Dante.

"Ta-da!"

Dante cocked his head at it. "I think we are too heavy to slide down it."

"No, no, it's not a slide." (Though, it wasn't completely unreasonable of him to compare it to one considering what I had to work with.) "It's a fort!"

"Oh, so you…" He looked to me to finish for him.

"…Can do anything you want! We could pretend someone is trying to infiltrate our base, or we can play shop and take turns being customers, or… well, what do you want to do?"

"Could we play… library?" He asked curiously.

"Sure! But… I mean, we do already have a library," I explained.

"How about bookstore, then? It could be called 'Inferno' because…" He pointed to himself. "And there could be a cafe, so you could have your sweets." With each new idea, Dante became undone with light, as if he was a shooting star. We pretended to ring up books and help customers find some rather hilariously crude titles. I made Dante an invisible coffee—extra hot with two sugars. He pretended to fire me (twice) for eating too many baked goods without paying. After we closed up shop for the day, Dante laid in my lap as I read to him. A poem about flowers. A poem about grief. A poem about birth. A poem about a Raven. It was strange how many lives could be lived in the one we all shared. It was stranger still how those memories affected the future, despite being an unchangeable part of the past. As I grew accustomed to the sound of my own voice, uncut off by others, Dante played with the hem of my dress, listening.

Nearing the end of the dozenth chapter, I had to clear my throat every couple of words to keep my voice from breaking. Eventually, that was no use. A sexy chainsmoker had possessed my ability to speak.

Dante sat up. "Would you like a glass of water?"

It itched attempting to make a joke about his chivalry, so I just nodded, rubbing my throat. Dante closed the door gingerly, leaving only for a few minutes before returning with a glass filled from the bathroom sink at the end of each hall. I gulped it down, and the glass grew foggy as I breathed into it.

Pulling the cup away from my mouth, water dribbled down my lips.

"Oh!" Dante leaned over instinctively, wiping the water away before it could drip onto my dress. I saw the realization surface through him in the red of his cheeks. "I…" He started to apologize, but his thumb didn't leave my lower lip, tracing it as he did his fingers. It slid smoothly over my cheek like it had always known the way. My heart started to beat as if it had never been at all.

The distance between us closed, and his lips brushed mine. They were soft, gentle, and…

Wet with saliva, like Bayle's tongue had been.

I jolted back, covering my mouth. The memory curdled inside my heart, heavy and unforgettable.

"I'm sorry. I'm sorry," Dante repeated profusely. "I—I didn't mean—I should have asked. I'm—"

"No, no," I replied, inching back to him, but still covering my lips. "It wasn't you. I just… it… I remembered when… *he*… I felt—" My gaze sunk to the floor, and I crossed my arms over my body, sheltering myself. "I don't know."

I had been so in tune, so focused on everyone else's emotions, I had forgotten mine.

Dante looked at me, ready to listen once again. He had already shared so much of himself with me. I guess I felt my experiences weren't bad enough to share.

"I have never kissed anyone before," I said to the ground. "The first time someone put their mouth on me was when Bayle…" I looked up at him. A shadow crossed his face as he remembered. I sensed anger festering inside of him, but the feeling quickly seceded as he took in my demeanor—hunched over, sunken brows, a frown full of realization about what had truly happened to me. He understood his rage wouldn't help.

"What can I do?" He asked.

What Bayle had done could not be changed. The suppression of my feelings after the fact was not something I could undo. Patience as I learned to listen to my own emotions was all I could ask for. "Stay," I replied.

"Blythe," he said. Solid red surfaced in his cheeks but with a squeeze of his eyes, he barged through it. "I would bury myself here if it meant I would always be with you."

My eyes welled with tears and I realized it was the first time I had let myself cry at Esalroth. They were tears of fear, but also joy. They were salty with anger, but also fun. I looped my pinky through his and we sat there.

We sat there until this would not be a memory of pain and confusion, but us.

Just us.

As Dante read one of his favorites— The Taiwanese translation of *Pride & Prejudice* by Jane Austen—while I lit candles, warding his room of evil spirits, three knocks boomed from halfway up on the door. I jumped up, heart racing, and pressed my body against the wall next to the door as Dante opened it, obstructing me from view.

"Tenold ditched us," Gus's voice said. A layer of his voice stumbled to control his indifferent demeanor.

"What do you—" Dante started.

Gus huffed out of his nose. "He *left* until 'further notice'."

The words held the weight and certainty of gravity.

The Headmaster had fled the school.

CHAPTER 23

After an immortal demon attack and our Headmaster abandoning us, Dante and I decided that relinquishing the rest of the day to rest may not be such a crime. I stumbled to my room and immediately slipped into my nightgown. Melsella didn't bother to ask questions, and frankly, I didn't care to answer.

The entire school had dinner carted to them that night and for the first. I could barely get halfway through my pasta.

We're-sorry-we-let-a-monster-into-the-school room service.

Please-ignore-the-fact-our-headmaster-ditched-you-all dinner in bed.

After stuffing myself with a meager amount of tomato sauce, the idea of shouting my condemnations to the sky—hoping they would reach wherever the Headmaster's ears were—was exhausted.

THE SON OF MARA

I had to conserve my energy in case the Son of Mara came to ensure I *really* stopped. That night, I stayed awake to the reverberation of my peers' panicked nightmares, feeling each one rattle in my bones to the point I could have sworn I caught glimpses of them.

A scorched paper molding into a beast made of lava with eyes the size of caverns that looked straight into hell.

The black courtyard clock enlarging until it swallowed a school whole.

Then, I felt a pluck of something like a raven's feather. Silky.

I reached out to it and smelled the leather of old books and the kindling of a fire. A girl laid out pastries and a boy shelved books. She beamed at him as if he hadn't given her the world—because it was not something for anyone to possess—but showed it to her. That was all. Sitting at a round cafe table, a short person and a tall person bickered over whether they should spend their last coins on a book about ancient dog bones or a slice of peach pie. The girl and the boy looked at one another and handed their friends their desired requests. In dreams, money was as unnecessary as waking up.

The dream continued in flashes, as though it had been a long time since the owner had dared to imagine. But the warm cotton of the dreamer's fulfillment tucked me in tightly, lulling me to sleep.

"THUD. THUD. THUD." A noise resounded from somewhere downstairs. I jolted awake, scrambling to my feet, already searching for a feeling to draw from. Student's dismay sparked as they each woke to the sound. Melsella sat up in her bed, arms ready to call on the worst hurricane to ravage sea and sky.

Our eyes met, and we inched toward the door, opening it slowly. I peeked outside. Some brave students leaned out of their doorway, looking around for a source. I turned back inside and plucked the lantern in our room from its hook. Creeping down the carpet, my bare feet felt the roughness of its age. Melsella kept behind me without a word while students gawked at us while we edged our way down the hall to the stairs. They followed at a generously respectful distance.

Delicate darkness shrouded the foyer, disturbed only by a yawning sconce or two. Melsella and I whirled our heads to the sound of whispers echoing from the school wing. We glanced at one another, needing only that one look to prepare to go down the hall.

I held the lantern up with one hand and spun the tingle of dread from my classmates in my other, then turned down the corridors. Our only guide was the occasional flicker of a lamp freshly lit. I braced myself for the possibility that this was it.

I would be fighting an immortal demon.

In my pajamas, nonetheless.

Digesting the unpredictability of the next few moments, I attempted to put some distance between Melsella and I.

You can't be so concerned with your surroundings, the Headmaster reminded me from afar. Though fury ensnared me when I even thought his name, he was right. He was still right. If she stayed with me, she could get hurt.

The whispers became audible as we peered down the dead end hall. The hallway with the Headmaster's office.

Three figures stood in front of his open door. From her satin bonnet to her navy robe, I exhaled in relief at seeing Professor Norwood. Beside her, a short and bald person with a pink head crossed their arms. Professor Sylmaris. Next to them, a man with a rusty beard and bushy eyebrows I recognized to be Professor Proudfoot—seasonal creaturology teacher.

"Professors?" I called. They startled, freezing with their eyes wide. "What's happened?"

"Miss Seraphin, Miss Melsella," Professor Norwood strode over to us. "Please go back to your room." She pressed a gentle hand to me, turning me back down the hall, but I broke away from her piloting.

"No," I stated. I felt Melsella tense by my side. The revelations and betrayal of the day—or, rather, yesterday—bubbled inside of me and spewed out on an unintended target. "You can't just train me for a battle and treat me like a child."

My words struck the Professor, her lips parting as if she had to open her mouth to be able to digest my words. She studied me and I could tell she was seeing a different Seraphin. Finally, she sighed, stepping aside for us.

We reached the end of the hall, Sylmaris and Proudfoot looked at us with solemn brows. Leading with my lantern, Melsella and I drifted inside, the damp cold infiltrating our nightgowns. Slashes marked the tapestries on the wall with ravenous movements. Shreds of sagas and legends trailed all the way to Tenold's desk, which now laid helpless on its side. His bookshelves and cabinets looked like they had been turned inside out. Files littered the floor as if they had attempted to flee.

An idea punctured the coolness of the room with sticky heat. I looked at the bookshelves once more, finding the only thing upright to be a hollow red cover. I shuffled closer. Before I so much as touched it I felt the lack of its daunting contents.

I pulled it out and opened its empty spine.

Not a shred of ink or parchment was left behind.

CHAPTER 24

"I don't understand," I said to the ceiling of the library, lying on the red sofa. "Why would he take the prophecy? It's not like he can change it."

Dante rubbed his chin, contemplating what felt like thin air.

The school day following had been a muddle of classes struggling to proceed with the chatter and questions of students.

Did the Son of Mara kidnap the Headmaster?

I heard Tenold was so stressed about the attack he's hiding in a bunker off the coast of Australia.

How did the Son of Mara get into the school?

He must have been helped by one of the monsters.

Why didn't Blythe stop him?

The thrum of emotions was so unbearable I told Professor Sylmaris I was sick before class could start. The fact *he* could be sitting in class with me, raising his hand, partnering with me in a group project caused me to prowl through the halls, feeling around for slick deception and spiraling vengeance. Eventually, I felt a strange buzz of excitement (for being in the school wing). I followed the fizzy thread of it and stumbled across Gus, Clyde, and Charlie playing cards in the empty planetarium.

"Sorry, I didn't mean to—" I started.

"Oh, don't be so modest, Blythe! Come play with us!" Clyde waved me over with her left pair of arms. Sitting in a circle under the stars, Gus threw his cards down. The blue tint the room gave made Gus' fit of anger look like a tiny angry shark's.

"Yeah, you-you should play," Charlie chimed in. "Gus n-needs someone else to lose to." Gus punched him in the arm, and Charlie rubbed the spot more to soothe Gus' ego than because of actual pain.

"Thank you, but…" I began to lie, and as wrong as it felt to deceive them, this was *for* them. This search was to protect them. They would understand. "I have a lot of work to do."

Clyde raised a perfect brow. "You don't have a study period now. You're supposed to be in… areas of lucid dreaming, right?"

Damn her attention to detail.

I clenched my fists together to keep myself steady. "Yeah, yeah, I'm just…" I walked backward towards the door. "Bathroom break." They all looked at one another, and I ran out the door. I released my pent up breath, putting my hands on my knees. I didn't even know why I lied to them. The whole reason I was at Esalroth was to defeat the Son of Mara.

My gut whispered something that frightened me—I knew they would disapprove of me cutting classes, searching, possibly overworking myself. I knew they would disapprove because it was wrong.

But, this had to be the right way. It was the only way to find him. To protect my friends.

"B-Blythe?" Charlie appeared behind me.

I drew my hand to my chest. "I didn't see you there."

Charlie shifted from side to side.

"I, um, didn't know you were friends with Clyde and Gus," I said, almost breathless with anxiety.

"W-we weren't until you showed them it was okay to be," he replied.

"Okay to be?" I repeated back with a raised brow.

He shook his head free from the topic. "I just wanna say that you shouldn't w-worry so much"

I stayed silent, feeling my shoulders tense.

"See, I came to Esalroth to prove that I could, b-but you don't have to do that!" He smiled. "Everyone already knows you can do it."

I gave him a half-smile to ease my words. "Defeating a demon is a whole lot different than being able to pass my classes."

He pressed his lips together, and knitted his brows. "You will run yourself ragged searching for someone who doesn't want to be found! You're m-my friend. I can't—I don't want you to end up…"

I placed my hand on his wrist, covered by the loose jacket he wore so dedicatedly, I could hardly picture him without it. His pulse thrummed under my fingers. "You're my friend too."

My heart heavier than before, I searched until the Bell rang for the end of the day. I now had one more thing to lose—to protect.

In the library, Dante asked, "Did Tenold have anything else of value?"

"Some procedure books, files, and tapestries, but he shredded up those pretty nice."

I felt like choice wasn't a guarantee but something orbiting farther and farther away from me. Deprived of sound sleep and sick of having things done *to* me, I sat up.

In my daze, I bumped into the coffee table, causing Dante to send a thick line of ink up the side of his homework.

"Gods below, I'm so sorry," I exclaimed, raising my hands as if I could suck the ink off the paper.

"It's okay. Sylmaris probably won't collect homework since we're spending most of our time reviewing occultism during the Medieval period. We're quite lucky, actually," he laughed to himself. "The Professor back then was brutal."

My cluttered thoughts snagged on his words.

"*The Looking Glass*," I remembered aloud.

"Yeah...," Dante eyed me like I should go back to lying down. "The one we use for all our—" His words caught, and realization sparked behind his eyes like a single candle struck in pure darkness.

"We can wheel it to the Headmaster's office and see who the Son of Mara is," I continued, my heart thumping against my chest. The Son of Mara felt so close I could smell the venom dripping off of him.

"How are we going to get it out of Sylmaris' room?" He asked.

I thought for a moment before a sharp grin cut across my face. "If time is money, we're about to cut it close to the penny."

<hr />

Dante and I snaked down the narrow stairway to classroom -66. The portraits' eternal gazes prickled the hairs on the back of my neck as we descended further. The Bell would ring for dinner in five minutes when Sylmaris would leave and lock the door.

But not before we propped it open.

The only problem was in a space so slim, there was nowhere to hide. So, we put Dante's ruined homework to good use. Dante yanked the classroom door open wide enough that it almost slammed into Professor Thrall's picture frame.

"Hi, Professor Sylmaris!" Dante sailed down the center aisle, averting their attention from the girl crawling through the door and under a desk.

"Mr. Shyung! The day is still young. It is good you have seized it before it wrinkled." Professor Sylmaris twinkled from their desk.

"Thanks, Professor!" His voice tripped over itself as it went so high.

"How March, April, May I help you?"

"You see, I happened to have had an unfortunate ink spill…" Dante explained his mishaps while I weaved through the chairs, trying to tuck myself in the farthest nook from the door as possible.

I could only hope the Professor didn't do a classroom sweep.

My very bones itched while waiting for the Bell to sound. The portal to the time this would all be over—the duels, the ceremonies, the *fear*—glistened only a few feet away from me and it exhausted all my restraint not to pounce up right now.

Before I could decide that maybe the idea wasn't *so* awful, the Bell rang three times, and Professor Sylmaris bounced up.

"There is no time like the present, and my gurgling stomach definitely considers this a gift," they said.

"Okay, well, thank you for understanding, Professor!" Dante squeaked, walking down the aisle with them toward the door. Suddenly, they stopped, and every muscle in my body constricted. They turned in my direction, surveying the area. I huddled in on myself farther.

"Do you smell that?" They asked.

"No, nope," Dante quavered. "Nothing in these nostrils." He breathed a laugh that surfaced the red in his cheeks.

"It smells like…" They sniffed the air. "Rue. An herb for exorcism and cleansing."

"Maybe… someone spilled it in class," Dante suggested.

"I must clean it up then!" They exclaimed, starting towards me.

"No!" Dante cried, startling the Professor. Drawing himself back in, he restated, "M-my friend, Blythe—I think she's in one of your classes—told me that when powerful herb's spill, it is because they have been called to cleanse the room. Best not to clean it up." He put his hands on his hips, nodding in agreement with himself.

Professor Sylmaris studied him and I had to cover my mouth to keep my breath from rising.

"Well, who am I to wrong such a bright witch?" They smiled, continuing with Dante to the door. "I would rather eat a hot potato than be one. Have a well-done or medium-rare dinner, Mr. Shyung!"

The door shut with a locking click as he uttered his thanks and I exhaled so heavily that if I were Melsella, the chairs would have blown over.

We decided Dante would wait five minutes before returning back down the stairs to help me lift the Looking Glass up the stairs. Staring at it, I realized it would be impossible to even fit through the doorway without breaking the legs off. Even then, hauling a mirror the size of a wall chalkboard would draw more than some attention.

I darted my eyes around, wondering if the Professor stashed a smaller version on her desk or behind the Looking Glass. However, what I did find would also be helpful—a bowl of what looked to be crushed up stars glimmered. I recalled the sparks leaping into the air as Professor Sylmaris clapped their hands and proceeded to use the Looking Glass.

This must be how you control it.

I dipped a finger in the bowl, rubbing the shimmer across my palm. I crossed back to the front of the Looking Glass and clapped my hands. The mirror awakened, reflecting just moments ago when Dante burst through the door and a mess of strawberry-blonde hair in a tan dress crawled past him. I grimaced at the fact my trespassing would forever be entombed in this mirror, able to be seen by any sneaky students and Headmasters alike.

Too late now.

I stared down the Looking Glass, unsure of how to proceed. "Show me… Monday." *My first day of classes.*

The mirror stared back at me.

"Please?"

The Looking Glass swirled around like a bubble mixture to reveal me, banging the door open, confused heads swiveling back to me.

A mirror that appreciates manners, I noted.

A light tapping came from the door. Twice, then a pause, then twice more. The code we agreed on.

I opened the door carefully, ducking my head to ensure no one followed Dante.

"We have a problem," I gestured to the size of the Looking Glass we had underestimated.

"Oh," he replied.

We walked up to it, studying it as if we could make it crack down to a reasonable size with our gazes.

"Okay, just promise you won't look," Dante said.

"What?"

He looked at the Looking Glass from the side, scrutinizing its surface. "You can brew a sealant, right?"

"Yes…" I followed where this was going but wasn't sure how we were going to get there.

"Vampires have some of the strongest teeth in creatures, so…" He looked at me to fill in the blanks.

"You're going to eat the mirror."

"I'm not going to eat the mirror!" He exclaimed. I chuckled at the way he always shook his head when he got frazzled. "I'm just going to chip off a piece big enough for us to use and then you can brew a sealant to fix it before anyone notices."

I extended my hand toward the Looking Glass. "Dig in."

CHAPTER 25

Dante and I left classroom -66 with a large shard of the Looking Glass in hand and Dante's shoe wedged between the door, so I could return to fix the mirror. I was sure it would have a word or two to say to us about the rudeness of biting objects.

Thankfully, everyone was attending dinner, leaving the hallways clear to roam into the Headmaster's office. Readying myself for the chill of the treacherous man's office, we stepped inside, shutting the door gingerly behind us. Every other sconce was left on from the professors' own investigations in the room. We took in the shredded path ahead of us.

Dante angled the mirror toward the tapestries and I raised my hands, eyeing the lingering dust sparkling in my palm.

I inhaled deeply, bracing myself. The face we might see in the mirror could be a classmate, a *friend*.

Before I could spiral any further, I clapped my hands together, sending sparks into the air. *"Please* show us last night."

The Looking Glass sputtered, working only as a fragment of itself. The pitch-black room the mirror reflected was lit by a single sconce. Dante fidgeted his hands, trying not to cut himself while also attempting to look at the image. The tapestry shredded before us was whole in this past world, doused in the dull light. Suddenly, lantern light spilled into the room. I worried I hadn't asked for far enough, but then the light lowered as if it was placed on the floor. I squinted my eyes, searching for a figure.

Suddenly, harsh lines dug into the tapestry, dragging it down to the floor. I took Dante's hand, pointing the mirror around, but no one was there. Then, a frenzy of torn fabric and thrown books flashed over the Looking Glass.

But no one was there.

It was as if everything in the room decided they had had enough and destroyed themselves.

"How is that possible?" I muttered, taking the mirror in my own hand and waving it around. "The Son of Mara might be able to shapeshift, but he can't turn invisible."

"Unless…," Dante wondered aloud. "Phantom creatures don't appear in mirrors. For Mara's last twenty years, she only turned herself into a poltergeist. What if she had a child with one? Mara and the poltergeist can shapeshift, giving the child the gene. But, no matter what form he shifts into, he will still be invisible in reflective surfaces."

"Gods below…" I ingested his words like I would a stone. I scanned over the room, the rabid destruction of it all. "Wait…" I sank down to the tattered tapestry on the floor, running my fingers over the rigid, *animalistic* tears. A harsh possibility surfaced in my mind. "What if… what if the Son of Mara wasn't in here at all?"

Dante raised a brow, and a part of me crumpled as I asked, "Can Gus," I swallowed hard. "Can he summon porquades?"

Dante recoiled back. "No, Blythe. No."

But that wasn't a response to my question—it was a response to the insinuation.

Porquades were phantom creatures formed from the flesh of bodies tossed to sea, leaving their skin looking blanched and shriveled. They're said to have talons the size of a dagger so they can crawl up from the depths of the oceans they were disposed of in.

"I know you care for him, but porquades can be called on by summoners." I began to paraphrase from my creaturology textbook, "In exchange for 'a taste of life', they'll comply with one command." *Could this be the command?*

"It's impossible for him to have attacked during the ceremony. He sat right next to me," Dante insisted.

"He didn't need to be in the clock tower. He could have sent a creature up there without even needing to move."

Dante shook his head. "Gus is… mischievous, but he isn't evil. He wouldn't…" His voice trailed off, finishing the sentence with a shake of his head.

"I know, I know, but," I searched for the right words to say to someone who felt so protective over this child. "But we have to at least talk to him. Like we did with Bayle."

"Gus is nothing like Bayle."

"You're right, so we shouldn't have anything to worry about."

I wanted to believe my words.

And right now, I had to force myself to as babbling spilled out from the dining hall.

Our time was up.

CHAPTER 26

As people began to stroll in for lunch, Dante and I lingered outside the dining hall doors. While we searched the flow of people for an overly dressed child with a plague doctor mask, I tapped my foot and gnawed on my lip. Guilt curdled inside of me for doing this to Dante. For even suspecting someone that I called a friend. Dante traced the knuckles of his hands with every passing moment, weaving in between each quicker than the last time.

I placed my hand on his. "We're only making sure."

He nodded.

"It could—"

Suddenly, someone gasped, and a rush of flowing clothes barreled into me.

"My Blythe!" Aunt Esther gushed.

Aunt Esther was here. In Esalroth.

I'm done for.

"What are you—" I started, but she shut me up with her welling hazel eyes and firm, searching grip on my shoulders.

"As soon as I got the letter about what happened, I came straight away. Are you hurt? Are you burned?"

She doesn't know about the letter from father, I realized. A moral test from him to see if I would choose by myself to do the "right" thing.

"I'm fine, Auntie. I promise." I looked around at the swarm of students pretending they weren't looking at us. "Let's go somewhere more private."

She nodded and I led her to two plush, warm-toned armchairs in the foyer. She ran her hands across the fabric, admiring it like it was something familiar. I looked her over for any signs of distress, but her strawberry-blonde hair was brushed neatly back in a ponytail—good, she wasn't neglecting her health—and her deep purple dress rippled off of her neatly—okay, she has been keeping up with the laundry.

I let out a relieved breath, finally able to let go of my father's cruel suggestion in his letter. My aunt was doing just fine.

"Why would a student play such a mean-spirited prank on you? Are you not making friends?" She asked, leaning forward with penetrating concern.

I raised a brow at her. Labelling what happened as a prank insinuated the Son of Mara was just a school-yard bully…

A realization stopped me cold. I had never heard of the prophecy until I came to Esalroth.

Aunt Esther has no idea.

"Who sent you that letter?" I asked.

"Your Headmaster."

Tenold had lied to my aunt and fled the school. The reason why he lied itched at me, and I was sure the truth would come to a blinding, harsh light soon, but for now, staring at my aunt's worried face, I couldn't help but be grateful. My aunt's eyes may have burst out of her head if she found out I was planning on defeating an evil demon sometime in the near future.

"Yes, Auntie. I'm making friends," I told her. "But I guess you can't be friends with everybody."

She cradled my face. "Good thing you don't need everybody."

I winced.

She had no idea.

The coolness of her rings against my skin felt like stepping into our home. It felt like hanging herbs brushing against my face, shared clothes now that I was old enough to fit her size, dirt under my nails from gardening, and the pages of second-hand textbooks. As she pulled her hand away, my mind stalled at what I saw on her pinky finger. At a glance, it would be easy to disregard the familiarity, especially amongst the dozen other, more decorative, rings jammed on her fingers. But the way it was worn in the same ways—black rust knicking away at it—as Professor Norwood's.

I pointed to it. "Where did you get that ring?"

She glimpsed down, pressing her lips together before saying, "Oh, um, it was just a friendship ring with someone from my school days." Her eyes traced the surface of the ring thoughtfully. "Though, I'm embarrassed to say it may have meant more to her than it did to me. See, Blythe, it's important to always make your intentions clear—"

"Did," I interrupted her. The way Professor Norwood twisted the ring absent-mindedly, thoughtfully, even after all this time. "Did she ever tell you how she felt?"

An emotion I could not quite pinpoint flooded Aunt Esther. The only feeling I could gather was the bone-aching soreness of it like a pressed bruise left abandoned by the healer of time. "Yes, but we had already graduated school by then and... I had met another." Her eyes trailed away.

My heart welled with even more guilt. Aunt Esther had a lover? Did she reject them because of her duties to me?

A burst of realization froze me over cold. Despite growing accustomed to the temperature with all the revelations occurring constantly, it dropped colder every time. Quick calculations in my head spiraled. Aunt Esther graduated from school about the same time I was born. Her jokes about how she almost fed me to the sheep for crying through the night slapped me in the face. Making the more than likely assumption that my father was away on business, and the certainty she was helping to raise me, meant the only person she would have 'met' was…

"Mom?"

Aunt Esther bowed her head, eyes darting around for a presence we both knew was countries away but *always* watching. Time and loss eroded away her ability to care. "Oh, it has pained me to not be able to speak of her with you," she gushed. "She would be so proud of how bright you are." Tears festered in her eyes, and the world felt like it was slipping from under me.

My mother. My nameless mother and my aunt rattled me.

"But dad—"

"Was away most of the time," she defended. "I knew a part of him suspected us, but he only ever cared about *having*. Not cherishing."

The man who thought *he*, the miracle worker, deserved the world. Did he separate them? Is that why my aunt was so dutiful in raising me? Not for her brother, but for her love?

My whole body was constricted. I squeezed the words out of my throat like old glue. "What was her name?"

My aunt smiled, caressing the name on her tongue. "Eve."

"Eve?" I tossed back. "But father's name is…"

"Adam, yes. Quite perfect, he thought."

The question that had been churning for so long dislodged itself and fell off of my tongue. Somehow both eager and hesitant. "What happened to her?"

She pressed her eyes together, pushing back the violent memories before they could consume her. "Your mom was a brilliant witch. She liked to experiment with new types of potions and spells, but one day…" She took a hollow, unsatisfying breath. "Something went wrong. She must have inhaled a soured concoction—practically a hallucinogen. She was raving about someone being after us—her, me, and you—and she told me we had to flee. She was so convinced she even bought us tickets to the ferry. It was selfish of me to believe her, thinking we could go live away together. With you. Because then—" She choked on the words. "Adam found her in the river." A tear escaped her eye, and she hastily swept it away. "If only I had stopped her, or—" She looked into my eyes, sobering her own expression. "It's okay. She's buried where they first met. She's happy there."

It sounded like she was reassuring herself more than me.

"I should have told you about her sooner. Your father just—he thought it would sting all the more knowing what a wonderful person you missed. A part of me felt the same way too. I'm so sorry, Blythe." The cool hand she placed on my knee froze me to my core.

An anger festered inside of me that had been kept dormant for reasons of not knowing. Not being certain I could even be angry. I pulled away from her. "Why did you follow what he said? Why have you always followed what he said? I could have grown up playing with actual children instead of sticks taped together to look like people. I could have *known her.*" I fumed, allowing the resentment to bubble.

"He would have taken you away with him! He would have taken the last piece of her." Her eyes reached out to me, to understand, to sympathize. But all I could feel was the stale anger they had hardened for too long.

"Did she even love you back?"

All the desperate emotions Aunt Esther bled tucked themselves away, and I instantly regretted the words.

"The last thing she said to me was 'I promise I'll come back to you'," she lamented, delicately brushing a hair behind her ear. "I see her in your intelligence, and your stubbornness, and your confidence. I'd like to believe she loved me enough to keep her promise, even after death."

"All this time, I thought I was holding you back from living," I admitted.

"Oh, no," she leaned forward, clutching my hands. "You're the very reason I do. I wasn't brave enough to tell your mother the truth, but I refuse to make that mistake again with you. Know I have loved you since the goddesses created you and I will even after they take you home. From now on, I promise I won't hinder your happiness. I will fight your father on it. "

I leapt into my aunt's arms. While she was always on my side, now we were a team, rather than a pair of mice running from a cat.

All this time I thought I had been missing pieces. A mother. A father. But a family wasn't labelled as such because of its size.

My father may love me from afar. My aunt loves me right here.

And my mother's love was untouchable inside of me. Breathing through my very lungs.

CHAPTER 27

After Aunt Esther and I said our goodbyes, promising to share more stories about my mother over break, I made my way back to the dining hall. I scanned the room but couldn't find Dante. Or Gus.

My heart quickened and I relinquished my grudge to the grey haired girl sitting in the front row. "Melsella," I said, tapping her shoulder. She looked up at me, surprised I was speaking to her. I was too. "Have you seen Dante?"

Her mouth twisted and she lowered her shoulders in disappointment she was poorly trying to hide. "No, why?"

Heat crept up my neck and lurched over my brow. I flicked my eyes across the room, hoping Gus would pop out from under the tables or Dante would peel himself from the shadows. "Nothing. But thanks anyways."

Melsella caught my disdain for her, rising from her seat. "I just wanted to say…"

"You're apologizing to the wrong person. *People*,

actually." I stormed away toward a more pressing matter.

There were only twenty minutes left of lunch, so I walked

as quickly as possible without raising suspicion. I started with the

library, checking behind each towering shelf in case...

Just in case.

Then I searched the courtyard that had started to become

littered with a mirage of vibrant red, murky orange, and sour

yellow leaves. A brisk wind kicked up, causing me to shiver.

A howl surged from the woods and jolted me paralyzed.

I bolted down to the paths, looking frantically between

each. My mind reeled trying to recall whether the sound came

from the left, or right, or semi-right...

Suddenly, my spirit reached out, pressing against my right

shoulder. I turned that way, holding my hand out. A feeling

shocked my system, too distant to identify, but icy and polar

enough that I sprinted so hard down the path, I was heaving by the

time I made out two figures.

No.

Three.

Trees encircled a plot of land that was caked in wet leaves

that stuck to one another. The path led to the center of the field.

Down to the left, Dante stood. Staring.

I turned in the direction and saw Gus clutching something

green in his hand. Another something stirred by his feet, reaching about his knees. Gus hurled the object towards Dante, and the figure beside him sprang forward into view.

A porquade.

No bigger than a baby bobcat, but as lethal as a supernatural tiger.

And it was running right at Dante.

"Dante!" I yelled, racing forward. "Move!"

He caught the item in his hands as he noticed me, sending a confused look. The porquade bounded into him, knocking him to his feet.

"Get it to stop!" I hollered at Gus. He only cocked his head at me. Maybe I imagined it, but I felt the sick smile forming under his mask.

I rushed over to Dante, drawing out my arm in search of the cold shock that led me here. I raised my hand, but as Dante's face came into view, it wasn't one molded by the chill of fear. Instead, it was the coolness that emanated from him as he laughed. A rumble that leaped higher the more the porquade licked at his hand, careful to keep its long talons on the ground beside him. Grasped inside of his palm was a simple tennis ball.

They were playing catch.

"In exchange for 'a taste of life', they'll comply with one command."

"Blythe," Dante caught my shocked expression.

"What…," My mind could not comprehend the scene. "What command is this for?"

"To get Xiomara to eat lunch," Gus replied. "Porquades have a hard time understanding how to *stay* alive." He rubbed his hand over Xiomara's ashen skin, and she nuzzled against his palm. Using the other hand, he reached into the line of his jacket pocket, pulling out a bag of what appeared to be cat treats. Xiomara turned her nose up at it. With a sigh, Gus knelt down beside her.

"You're lucky you don't stink as bad as the hellhounds." He unstrapped his mask and placed it on the ground.

I was never more pained to be right. Gus could only be about twelve years old. A twelve year old with two scars tearing across his lips like an "X".

This was not a face that was hiding an immortal demon —it protruded a weathered and worn childhood all too well.

Xiomara swiveled her head back around and licked his face happily before smacking on the treats.

Gus looked up at me, and it occurred to me I hadn't stopped staring at his scars. I turned my face away.

"They didn't do this to me," he replied, referring to the creatures. The edge to his voice had softened, but not faded. Xiomara finished her food, then she laid her head on Gus' knee, comfortable enough to take a rest after her meal. "They are more family than the people who did."

Dante lowered his head, bearing the weight of Gus' hidden pain for him. It hadn't occurred to me until they stood side by side that Gus' all-black suit resembled Dante's own wardrobe. I was sure if anyone pointed it out he'd deny it, but I was glad that Gus had found someone else to call brother.

Pulling his mask back on, he added hastily, "And I don't wear my mask because I'm ashamed. I wear it to—"

Gus said, "Intimidate" at the same time, Dante said, "Look cool." Gus crossed his arms, but didn't deny Dante.

"Xiomara was in Clyde's room the night someone broke into Tenold's office. Clyde has nightmares and finds the company helps her sleep." He stroked Xiomara's head and she gave a hum. "If the porquade had left, she would have woken up." And summoners can only call on one creature at a time. I breathed a sigh of relief. *It wasn't him.*

"I shouldn't have assumed—" I started. Gus held up his hand, his brown eyes still, but not silent.

"I only tell you because I want him caught," he stated. "So mistakes like this don't happen again."

Bayle, Melsella, and now me. I had looked down on them so harshly only to realize I was one of them too. I slept in unnecessarily large dorms and was treated as if I could do no wrong.

Gus never owed me kindness. I only expected it because that's what I had ever been exposed to, people who swore I was the best person alive without exchanging a single word with me.

Gus was not evil. He was a person, a *child*, who had experienced the harshness of life in such a short one. A child who had endured cruelties I was not entitled to pry from him. The most I could do was help make this life more bearable as much or as little as he would let me.

"You have my word."

CHAPTER 28

Two weeks. Fourteen days (or was it thirteen? fifteen?).
An agonizing two weeks went by without a whisper from the Son
of Mara—or the Headmaster. Every night, I stayed awake, fueled
by the steady ripple of nightmares from my classmates. Each day,
I monitored my peers for a deceptive word, a sneaky movement, a
jagged feeling that was misplaced amongst the rest. One only he
and I would share.

Waiting.

Dante had forced me down to the library to complete
the homework I already received an extension for—twice. I bit
my nails as I tried to make sense of the letters that were supposed
to form words but computed in my brain as well as mush. The
commanding presence of the shelves surrounding us whispered to
me to continue searching for the spines of journals or books about
Mara. *Just one book. Just one peek. Just look. Come, come look.*
You need to check. Just a glance.

214

Maybe we're missing something, I thought as I gnawed on my nails. *Maybe we should search again. If we—*

A sharp sting pricked my finger. My nail was bleeding.

I gazed at the beds of my nails, circled with aggravated blisters at most two weeks old. Now all of my fingers were ensnared by them.

I narrowed my eyes at Dante, who sat across from me, scribbling over his work with ease. I licked over the blood and forced my attention back to my notebook. Mindlessly bouncing my leg up and down, and up down, updownupdownupdown, I flipped the pages back in search of the answer to an alchemy question, but the prophecy I had written over, and over, and over again seized me by the neck and pulled me straight down.

The lines churned in my mind.

The Son of Mara shall return to fulfill his mother's wrath.
The one to save all must be led down the right path.
As one grows stronger, so shall the other.
But the power of the chosen one will make all stutter.

The path. Was it a physical one? Like the ones leading out into the woods? Or a metaphorical one? Like I should be training with Professor Norwood instead of telling her I had too much homework to do?

THE SON OF MARA

I held my head in my hands. If one grows stronger as the other does, the Son of Mara is in a real slump.

One side of the arched door kicked open, sending a boom echoing through the room that caused even the books to startle. A tall ray of yellow, black, and white burst through the room toward us. Disrupting her color palette, a crimson dress swayed in Clyde's hands. The dress of my dreams existed with a neckline that fell below the collarbone and extended to the edge of the shoulders. Short puffed sleeves dripped with white lace. The waist tightened around the ribs and floated out into a crinoline silhouette.

"I knew I would find you two here!" She congratulated herself, peering down at us. Then, she took my wrist, noticing my fingers. "I have always prided myself on my timing."

"We're trying to finish our homework," Dante said. I glanced over at his notebook and saw he was doing the homework for tomorrow. He was stalling for me to finish my own from days ago. Guilt pulled at my insides.

"Spectacular! This will cheer you up then!" She raised the dress out to me.

"Clyde—" My breath caught as my eyes spun with stars. "What about your dress? I thought you were worried you wouldn't be able to make it in time."

She snapped her right pair of wrists with an *oh please*. "I have time."

"It's in three days!" I reminded her.

"You worry too much," she smiled, pushing back her hair. "Gus' spindelettes can help me."

Spindelettes. Creatures as thin as a needle who spun fabric for the devil himself.

"Thank you, but—I'm sorry if this is rude—why?" I asked.

Dante and Clyde exchanged a glance. "Your sacrifice doesn't go unnoticed," Clyde said.

I buried my fingers under themselves. Took in the dress. Took in Clyde, Dante.

I barreled into Clyde with a hug. Measuring five inches shorter than her, I wrapped my arms around her torso as her top pair of hands nestled around my neck.

Clyde tossed the dress to me as if it were as easy to come by as a dandelion. Taking my seat, she pretended to grow sick at our heap of homework. Her eyes lit up as she read the pages spiraling with the words of the prophecy.

A giggle bubbled out of her. "The copy Tenold has is not nearly as impressive as the original, in my opinion."

Dante and I's hearts skip a beat at the exact same moment.

"The what?" I blurted out.

"The original! I'm one the few who's actually seen it," she boasted. "I'm not sure why he stores it where he does. Protection, probably. Yeah," she agreed with herself, nodding. "Probably smart after the whole break-in."

Frayed rope coursed through my veins, both persistent and paralyzing. The thread of suspicion coming from the Headmaster had been pulled taut for two weeks. But right then, I felt it give. "Where is it?"

"A pretty clever spot, actually," Clyde replied, casually flipping through my notebook. Dante and I stared at her so eagerly I felt the electricity sparking through our gazes. "The Bell tower."

"There is no Bell tower," Dante asserted.

"Not one that you can see from the ground." Clyde winked.

Clyde paraded out to the front of the school while Dante and I scampered behind her. Fall wind rushed around me, dancing through air as I stared out at the world from behind the gates of Esalroth. I anticipated a pang of strangeness, but all I felt was the familiarity of my friends beside me like this was the right way to view the world.

"Sorry, Danny. I may have four arms, but they are quite weak. I can only carry one person," Clyde said.

"Wait, carry?" I bawked out. I only got a glimpse of Clyde's wings that fanned out to span her arm length before she turned me around, closing her arms over me.

"We won't be long!" She exclaimed, and before I could utter a word of protest—or prayer—we soared into the air. The clouds became larger, and the trees pricked with orange and red stood at our height.

Until they shrank.

It would not be a far-fetched guess to have said Clyde was showing off—sailing far above the height of the school—but as we shot across the sky like an afternoon star, the gravity weighing me down tumbled to the miniature world below. If Clyde let me go, I could have sworn I would not have fallen but landed amongst the clouds.

"What could ever make you come down after a view like this?" I joked, shouting to be heard over the wind rocketing past us.

"Not a what. Who," she shouted back.

The memory of the leather spine on a book about Rome and the cloth of the recordings from Italy felt artificial in my hands compared to Clyde's tender grip and the awe teeming from Dante down below. Maybe the destination I yearned to go to was not a place but a person. People. While the idea of seeing the wonders of the world enchanted me, maybe the location was not as important as the people accompanying me.

We weaved through the spires and domes of Esalroth, sometimes coming close enough I could drop my feet and skitter across the rooftop. Finally, we closed in on a cluster of towers I recognized from the view to be some of the classrooms. As we circled around the shortest one of them all, Clyde slowed down to scan the surface.

"Clyde?" I asked.

"Hm?"

"If you ever need me to, I wouldn't mind sleeping in your room. Or you could come to mine since it has two beds." I felt her grip loosen on me before she realized she was the only thing keeping me from falling. "I don't mean to be intrusive. It's just Gus mentioned it and… I just… I don't know. I've never done 'friends' before and I want to get it right, but if that's too much—"

"It is more than enough." She held me tighter. Then, sighing, she said, "Being here, at Esalroth, well, I won't go out of this world the same way I came into it. Before here, I never knew of cotton sheets, and lights, and meals you did not have to fight for." I felt her shiver, though, not from the cold. "While the past may plague me at night, I find the day. It always comes, so why worry?"

"Ah!" Clyde cheered to one of the stones. She tightened

her grip around me as she reached out with one arm and pressed against the stone. As she pushed harder, an outline of a small door began to form. Small fragments of the wall sputtered out as if it had been a long time since its last opening. Clyde gave a final shove, and the door budged open, revealing a dark room that smelled of must. She lowered me inside before fluttering back. She would not fit through the door with her wings extended, so she flew straight at it and closed her wings at the last second, sending her tumbling through the room until she hit something that made a familiar *dong* sound upon impact.

The room was only visible through the daylight filtering through the open door. A golden mass shivered behind Clyde as she stood up, rubbing her head. *The Bell.*

"Not the nicest place to keep it," she said as I took in the cobwebs knitting themselves on every surface.

"Homier than Tenold's office at least," I replied.

Clyde ducked under the Bell. Only her black heels were visible from the outside.

"Here it is!" Her voice echoed loudly. She popped back out from under the Bell and handed me a piece of paper in no better condition than the one from Tenold's office. If anything, it looked as hastily written as notes for a teacher who talks too fast. The most damning difference between the two though, were the words… written in an unfamiliar language. I pulled out a scrap piece of paper and a whittled down pencil from my pocket. Besides the note that tomorrow I had a seasonal zoology quiz I now could not possibly study for, I copied down the words from an alphabet I didn't recognize. I handed the paper back to Clyde, and she returned it to its tucked away position.

"Let's get out of here before the Bell rings for dinner, and we go deaf," I said.

Clyde, Dante, and I attempted to decipher the origin of the alphabet as we walked back into the library, only to collide with a flurry of grey hair.

"Watch where—" Melsella stopped when she recognized me. "Oh. Blythe. Sorry."

"It's fine," I replied, going to move past her, but she took hold of my wrist, looking at the paper clutched in my hand.

I yanked my arm away.

Her brows quirked. "What are you reading in Old Norse?"

Old Norse? I had not given much thought to the country the prophecy originated from, but I was not expecting Norway. I held up the paper. "Can you read this?"

"Of course. I know over a dozen languages. Ancient and modern," she beamed.

I looked uncertainly at Dante who shared my same feeling. Before I could evaluate the risks of trusting Melsella, Clyde stole the paper from my hands, replying, "Thank you, Mel."

A faint blush nipped at *Mel's* cheeks as she took the paper from Clyde's hands. She read it over, furrowing her brows as she recognized the text. "Is this supposed to be the prophecy?"

"It is the prophecy," I corrected her.

"I'm trying to learn ancient languages," Dante lied, overcorrecting.

"Well, it's pretty good except for this first part." She pointed to the first line. "You wrote 'Child of Mara' not 'Son of Mara'."

I went numb as my breath hitched. I snatched the paper from her as if I could prove she had misread it. "Are you sure?"

"Yes, he wrote '*barn*', or child, instead of '*sonr*' which means son." Her words plummeted into my brain as she spoke to Dante. "Also, you might want to work on your handwriting."

I paced over to the nearest chair and collapsed into it. All this time, I had been focusing on the male students. Every night I had been concentrating on the boys' dreams in case one was laced with a nauseating vengeance. Each day I had pinned them down with my scrutinizing gaze. *All this time*, crucial information had been dismissing us from class and ushering us to meals. My suspect list went from a little less than half the school population to all of it with just one word.

THE SON OF MARA

The hidden prophecy. The fleeing. The lying. The threads chasing the Headmaster wove up the back of my throat, forming into bile.

CHAPTER 29

The end of the week came with enthusiastic chatter about the Hallow's Eve ball commencing in two days. Students discussed their attire while hauling elaborate decorations to and fro. I tried to participate in the excitement, but all I could do was look over my shoulder. Each person that glimpsed a second too long or brushed past me a little too harshly sent my hairs on end.

By the end of the school day, I retreated to the safety of my room. I anxiously drew the curtains, so I didn't have to keep an eye on my window too. Clyde and Dante had to coax me out with the promise they *both* would ask Chuck for a side of taffies. While we descended down the foyer staircase, Clyde raved about the efficiency of the spindelettes. Relief absolved my guilt over her generosity when she informed us that she would be able to finish sewing the dress by tomorrow at the rate they were spinning. As Dante was talking about the history of balls—telling us that the waltz was invented as an excuse for fairies to move at their natural quick pace—the front doors swung open. The commotion of students came to a halt.

Looking as rejuvenated as ever, Headmaster Tenold walked through the doorway. Every restless day, every sleepless night over the past two weeks boiled inside of me. He had abandoned us at the first true sign of a monster, and he dared to stroll in here as if he just came back from vacation?

I stormed down the stairs and straight towards him. When I caught his attention, anger surged through me. He looked *pleased*.

"Miss Seraphin! How are you doing? Is training going well?" He asked, a *smile* lining his thin lips.

"I could be better," I retorted. "I would have preferred to hide in a demonless place as well, but I guess my responsibilities outweigh yours."

The students surrounding us gasped. The Headmaster's face sank into the stoic cast of a man I remembered him to be.

"Mind yourself, Miss Seraphin. My business does not need approval from a student," he returned with a voice as undisturbed as stone.

I brushed him off, shooting back, "I found the original prophecy. You mistranslated it. It's not 'the *Son* of Mara'. It's 'the *Child*'."

The color drained from his face, leaving the bare bones of the structure he held so apathetically. "That's not possible." The words left his throat in a petrified hiss.

"Yes, it is. I checked it."

Goddesses above, Melsella, please don't make me look like a fool in front of the entire academy.

"I transcribed it myself," he breathed. The room went silent.

"No," I murmured. "That prophecy is ancient."

"Only as ancient as I," he replied. He hardened his composure, knowing I would not back down. He opened himself to the foyer, announcing to all, "I come from a family of Vikings and Norse practitioners from the Isle of Man. When I was no older than Miss Seraphin, my family exorcised Mara herself." Hushed whispers splintered through the delicate tension in the air. "I was too young to fight myself, so I stayed with my grandmother. Moments before my family vanquished Mara, my grandmother foretold the prophecy you all know today before she walked into the battle zone, leaving me the last remaining Tenold."

The room stilled, the words cementing in widened eyes.

He turned back to me, eyes unfeeling. Empty. "Forgive me for mistranslating a word in my grief."

"But… but—" Something still wasn't making sense. The fleeing. The lying—

THE SON OF MARA

"Blythe, watch out!" I heard Clyde cry, followed by a crunch from above and a whur hurtling down towards me. As a blur of flying black, white, and yellow knocked me back, I saw a large, splintering piece of the second-floor balcony mantle crush Clyde in my place.

A shrill wail consumed every sound. I rushed over to Clyde, Dante meeting me from the other side. We pushed the debris off of her, revealing her agonized face, streaked with tears.

And her wings, which were now torn.

Bile lunged up my throat. I clasped my hands over my mouth. A curious swarm of students started circling us, all recoiling back in horror as soon as they saw Clyde's shredded wings.

"Headmaster!" Melsella cried, having already pushed her way through to Clyde's side. "How do we carry her to the infirmary? Should I go fetch the—"

The Headmaster silenced her with a raised hand, his face completely detached as if he could not hear the agonized cries of his student. "That is not necessary, Miss Melsella. Miss Seraphin can heal her."

Blood drained from my face at the sound of my name. The weight of his request. "S-sir, I've never dealt with something so complicated before." I didn't even think Aunt Esther had, or else she would have taught me. Moths' wings weren't sturdy like bone. They were even more delicate than paper and couldn't mend in the same ways as skin. On top of that, Clyde's wings didn't just have a small slice—like a fairy might get in harsh woods—but entire pieces were torn off that would need to be reattached. And with the state they were in…

"There is no need for false humility. You see—" He began to say, but a scream blared from Clyde, tearing through his words.

"Headmaster, please!" Melsella pleaded, overwhelmed with such raw emotion it gargled in my throat. I had never been so overtaken by another's feelings so much so that it constricted my breathing. "She needs to go to the infirmary!"

Tenold stepped towards Melsella, side-stepping Clyde as she writhed in agony. "It is one thing to question my judgment." Melsella shrank as the Headmaster stepped closer, his words cut sharper. The purple of the bow she had pinned to her bodice seemed to fade. "But it is an entirely different thing to question *the one*'s abilities. Is that what you are doing?"

"N-n-no, Headmaster. I just—" She sputtered.

"This is very unlike you, Miss Melsella. Your parents would be very displeased."

The anguish suffocating me was sucked out as Melsella shrivelled into herself.

"Miss Seraphin," the Headmaster turned to me, his face lit by the barest sliver of what I feared to place as excitement at the opportunity. "Will you please help Miss Chaumont?" He said it as plainly as if he was requesting I tutor Clyde in creaturology.

Move, my spirit whispered.

I sprinted to my room, frantically gathering every jar of mine I could hold. Then, I ran back down the stairs two at a time, stumbling to the ground beside Clyde. Dante held her hand as she wept while Gus barked at people to move back or he would use their toes as dominoes.

Kneeling, I dropped the jars beside me and assessed the damage. The rest of her looked unharmed, so I focused my attention on her wings.

"Find the rest of her wings!" I instructed Dante, Gus, Melsella, anyone. We searched the ground, finding fragments of it thrown across the floor or punctured through the wood's jagged thorns. I laid the frail pieces on the ground, trying my best to make the frayed edges fit together. My blisters yelped in pain while I cut herbs with my fingernails as best I could. I ripped the cork off the jar with my teeth, mixing agrimony in my hand as a makeshift bowl. Finally, I poured an unmeasured amount of honey into my palms.

Cut, and mix, and pour. Clyde yelled, low and guttural. *Cut, and mix, and pour*. Clyde choked on her tears.

"It's okay," I fretted, desperately trying to make the sealant latch onto the jigsaw puzzle I had on the floor. Heat slithered up my spine. That was only a part of her wing. After that, I still had to make that piece take to the wings still attached to her body.

She sobbed, her cries, raw and blistered, punctured my brain and stung my eyes.

"It's okay," I quavered. "I'm going to fix it."

Cut, and mix, and pour.

"I'm going to save you."

I doused the pieces in the sealant, hoping they would hold together. Then I gently coated the torn edges of the wings still attached to her body. I breathed as that seemed to edge off the pain, her cries subsiding.

I turned back to the puzzle of her wings. Hope thrummed from my fingers as I slid them under her wings, praying to every goddess, god, and otherwise they would weld together.

I lifted it, and the pieces crumbled apart.

"No," I gasped. "No, no." I pushed the pieces back, drenching it even more sealant. I tried again. The pieces fell to the ground like an infant bird out of a tree.

Whispers hummed in my ears from the crowd around us. Their bodies hovered over me, towering taller than the shelves in the library, higher than the spires of the academy. Their eyes dug into me. Layered beneath the horror, there was judgment. Fear that I couldn't do this.

THE SON OF MARA

"If I remember correctly, you do not need aids to do witchcraft," The Headmaster interjected.

Hands trembling, I held them over Clyde's wings, searching for any feeling delicate enough to touch them with. *Pain. Fear. Disgust. Misery. Anger. Shock. Fear. Fear. Fearfearfearfearfear.*

Consuming of the soul and penetrating of the heart, fear.

Whispers whispered whispers. *She couldn't do it. She's been a witch her whole life, and she couldn't do it. She received all the extra training, all that extra help, and she failed.*

She can't save us.

"I—" I whimpered, inching back. The eyes of the crowd followed me, wrinkling their noses, mouths turned down in revulsion. I met Clyde's eyes. The yellow of them were glassed over like a porcelain dandelion about to shatter.

"I'm sorry," I breathed, tears pressed against my eyes. I stumbled back and dashed out the door.

CHAPTER 30

The sound of Dante calling after me ricocheted in my mind as I raced into the woods, unsure of where to go, uncertain of what to do. I panted the evening fall air, each breath slicing my throat, over, and over, and over. Low hanging branches fought my advances, cutting my face with their shadowed limbs.

Clyde's yellow eyes flashed across my vision. A comet burning, fading.

I fell on my knees and let out dry, painful sobs. My chest heaved as my fingers dug into the cool ground, searching for anything. Anything to fix the mess I made.

I couldn't stop the Child of Mara.

I wasn't diligent enough.

I wasn't focused enough.

And now he's hurt one of the people I love most.

All because of you, a voice hissed from a place I didn't know.

THE SON OF MARA

I should have trained harder.

I should have searched longer.

I should have sensed their presence. They were *right above me.*

And I didn't feel a thing.

If I had never come to Esalroth, the Child of Mara would have remained as weak as I was—just like the prophecy said.

I screamed into the dimming sky ripping my throat until the copper taste of blood spat into my mouth. How selfish was I? I was hunting the child of a demon who had destroyed countless cities and I recruited the help of people I hadn't even known for a full month.

My stomach turned. I had asked Dante to help me the first day we met.

I roped them in too far, and now they were suffering because of me.

In my place.

The Child of Mara meant to crush *me*, not Clyde.

And I dared to say I was here to save them?

The chill of the wet leaves crept up my hands and into my bones.

It was too late now.

I sat up, wiping the remnants of the damp fall ground on my dress, smearing it with dirt. I wiped my eyes with the backs of my shaking hands.

If I was going to have it all, if I was going to have friends, or a life lived without paranoia dictating my every move, I was going to finish this.

I would lure the Child of Mara out and defeat them before they could so much as breathe on my friends again. Or I would perish trying.

CHAPTER 31

I holed up in my room for the night, unable to stomach even the thought of dinner. When Melsella returned for bed, she told me Clyde was physically fine since her wings had no veins or bones in them. *Physically* fine. I had seen her face while we soared over the world, unable to be touched by any worry or plight.

She would never know that again.

The following day, I stayed in my bed until Melsella brought me a bowl of strawberries from breakfast. Even then, I could only get as far as my desk. I asked her to leave so I could be alone with my thoughts. She agreed only on the condition that I would come to lunch. I accepted.

I lied.

That day, I would prepare for the Hallow's Eve Ball tomorrow. Not by ironing out my gown or trying on different hairstyles, but by devising a plan to draw out the Child of Mara and lead them outside, away from everyone else. Then, I would vanquish them for good.

Practicing outside would have been more ideal, given I would have less to catch aflame or smash into a million pieces. However, I refused to risk the chance of Dante, Gus, or Clyde—if she wasn't in the same state I was—running into me. I allured any and all danger, and I swore they would never be within breathing distance of it again.

I spent the afternoon practicing by drawing from my own emotions. A torrid anger erupted from my palms, bursting a strawberry into oblivion. Revolting hate drummed through my arms as I punched out holes in one of my dresses I stuffed with a pillow. Guilt rippled off of me as I tore the pillow in two with only so much as a head nod.

I slumped down, every vengeful feeling pumping through my veins. I felt shrivelled and overflowing at the same time.

A gentle knock sounded. Twice. Then a pause. Then twice more.

"Blythe, it's Dante,"

I flinched at the wrinkle in his voice. The concern.

"We just want to check on you."

We.

No, they can't all stay here.

The Child of Mara could wipe them all out at once.

I held my breath, hoping they would think Melsella took me for a walk or something.

"Blythe, are you in there?" He asked again, his voice bleeding lower.

"If you don't say something, we're gonna think you're dead, and then we'll have to break the door down," Gus piped in. "Melsella would send a category six."

I pressed my back against the frame of my bed to keep from trembling. I winced as it let out a creak.

"Blythe…" A voice I could only hear as yellow said. "I'm okay. The cream you used kept it from getting infected. They feel —" She hesitated. "Fine. They're okay. So am I."

I pressed back tears.

"I would do it again if I had to."

"No," I shouted back. "You need to stay away from me until I fix this. I'm going to fix this. I'm going to stop it all."

"Blythe—" Dante started.

"LEAVE!" I bellowed, the words tearing through my heart before they did my throat.   Three pairs of feet shuffled down the carpet as a cry that barreled through my ribs and constricted my brain heaved itself out in stifled, silent screams.

I pulled myself into the crimson gown, grateful its length covered my brown boots. Melsella insisted on curling my hair by way of heating her hands over the fire and then twirling my hair with hot gusts of wind. The end result left me looking like a fairytale princess with half of my hair tied back and the rest left in loose ringlets spilling over my shoulders. I might have enjoyed the process if I wasn't constantly checking the window in our room to make sure nothing, or no one, was about to hurtle through.

"You go on ahead," I told Melsella as the sun started to set and the Ball was about to begin. "I just want to fix my makeup."

I had never worn makeup in my life.

She hesitated but nodded, tightening the bow in her hair before she went to leave.

"Wait," I said even though my every cell told me not to keep anyone near me for too long. But the reminder that the Child of Mara was just as powerful as I was resurfaced in my mind. If this was my last night…

"It was you who said we have to dress like a formal version of *ourselves*," I pulled the purple bow she had forsaken to the trash after the night of Clyde's injury from my chest. Melsella looked wary but turned around. I untied the bow and wrapped the fabric around the waist of her white gown that trailed behind her.

"Well… I guess I can't break those rules," Melsella conceded. She went to leave again, but stopped. I swallowed hard. "Blythe?"

THE SON OF MARA

I was sweating now. *She's been too close to me long enough.*

"Hm?"

She pressed her lips together before revealing the emotions I had felt developing inside her for some weeks. "How do you know if you like someone?"

I was a bit taken aback, stuttering in reply. "Um, I…. I don't know. I've never—well, no, I mean, maybe…" My cheeks felt like coals were burning under them.

Melsella shrunk into her shoulders, waving her hands in front of her, smiling to conceal her embarrassment. "Forget it. It was a silly question."

"No, no." I scolded myself for giving her another opportunity to stay with me, but I pressed on. She was my… roommate. Roommates did this sort of thing—I think. "Well, I suppose… love is silent. It's not butterflies flapping mercilessly around in your stomach. It's more like… you're constantly drawn to them, and them to you. Like a moth to the light."

Melsella perked up, then, smiling to herself, "A moth." Her full brown eyes looked into mine, and it was the first time I had seen Melsella. Not Melsella, distant relative of Aeolus. Not *Miss* Melsella. Just, Melsella.

Mel.

She threw her arms around my neck, embracing me in a hug that consumes you, body and soul.

"Don't step on her dress," I said into her hair. "She worked hard on it." Melsella pulled back, twisting her lips to keep from smiling instead of frowning at my cheekiness.

I pinned up my smile until she shut the door. I inhaled a breath that stuttered on its way to my lungs. My plan was risky and possibly expulsion-worthy, but right now, it was all I had. The Child of Mara first attacked when I displayed my power. Tonight, I would stand in front of the great window—pushing everyone as far back as I could—and give them a show Mara's child couldn't resist destroying. Then, before the Child could hurt anyone in the room, I would smash the window open and lead them outside.

Then, I wouldn't just defeat them. I would annihilate them.

Not easy, smart, or clever, but I refused to wait until they struck again.

CHAPTER 32

The cafeteria had been converted back into a ballroom.
The red satin tables were replaced with the twirling skirts of
dancing students. Roses climbed the ivory columns, spattering the
golden aura of the room with a deep red. The chandelier above it
all seemed to twinkle even brighter, invigorated by the silks and
velvets sashaying below. Below the Palladian window, a
symphony entranced the room with the flow of violins, a crash of
drums, and whine of trumpets. I would have to disband them into
the crowd before I lured out the Child of Mara, or their
instruments would sputter only glass.

I snaked through the pairs of waltzing students, side-
stepping here and lurching there in order to not knock into them
or be knocked into. I ducked behind another couple when
Melsella and Clyde came twirling through. Clyde's dress streamed
off of her like a thin veil of night, bedazzled with yellow
gemstones. At her waist, a layer of firm white fabric curved off of

her like she was stepping out of a cocoon. As Melsella spun her, Clyde's frayed wings became visible. A pang of remorse was quickly snapped up when I saw the look on Clyde's face while dancing with Melsella. Weightless. Free.

And here I was ruining their evening again. I choked down the heaviness crawling from my chest to my throat, coming to consume my thoughts, my actions. This was for *them*. For their safety. There would be other balls, but not other lives.

I made it to the center of the room before fingers like piano keys pulled my waist. A tumble of shadows in an all black suit grabbed my other hand, leading me in the dance.

"How were the strawberries Melsella brought up?"

"Dante, you need to get away from me," I returned, trying my best to not trip over my own feet.

He smiled back. "We said we were going to do this together."

I flicked my gaze down, unable to bear how his eyes reached out to me, hoping, hurting. There, in his breast pocket was a red pocket square—like he intended to match with his… me.

If you cared for him, you would protect him. All of them, I scolded myself.

My anxious grip tensed on his shoulder, allowing me to feel the muscle hidden beneath. "No, you said you were going to help me research Mara. I never should have let you help me with the rest."

"I don't think you could have broken the Looking Glass with those human teeth, no offense."

I shook my head. How could he not comprehend the gravity of this situation? "You need to get away from me before something bad happens again." He extended his arm up, spinning me around. When I faced him again, I forced out what I knew would stop him. The truth. "Dante, I am like the sun to you."

His twinkling eyes sobered at the words, like a sky drained of its stars. He let go of my hands and my waist, leaving us two statues surrounded by an array of gilded motion.

"I have something you need to see," he said solemnly.

I hesitated at the idea of leaving the entire school alone, a mass unprotected target.

"If it doesn't satisfy you, I will leave you alone." The darkness of his eyes stilled. A river made bottomless by midnight. "For good, even."

I felt Dante's confidence fortify him, sure enough to take the risk.

I nodded.

Dante led me down the way to the courtyard, but instead of going through the door, he walked right past it. Rounding another corner, we stopped at a simple wooden door I had passed dozens of times, assuming it was a broom closet. He opened it and a spiral of stone steps awakened in the darkness from the light in the hall. With one hand, I hiked up my dress to keep from tripping. With the other, I held on to the wall, needing the support for the steep journey. The only guide to us was the subtle glow from a light up above.

We climbed for about five more minutes before we reached the top. The wheel shaped mechanisms and cogs told me where we were before I needed to ask.

The clocktower.

"After what Tenold told everyone, I remembered what you said about the Child of Mara taking the copy of the prophecy. Why? Why take something you can't change?" Dante walked backwards as he spoke, the old floorboards creaking with each step. "Unless that's not the only thing they took."

Sitting on the floor in the corner, I noticed what illuminated the room. A lantern in the same style as the ones issued in our rooms. "They knew they couldn't hide it in their room after how they searched us, so where else could they hide it? Where else could *they* hide?"

Dante stepped down on the end of a floorboard and the other side lifted up like a seesaw. Inside was not just the folded up copy of the prophecy, but a manilla folder. The same kind that was scattered around the Headmaster's office. The kind that contained information on students.

They had stolen their file.

I opened it and almost dropped the file upon seeing the picture.

"*Charlie?*" I gaped. "That's not possible. He's an ogre. He's not magical. He—" I read the first line.

Age: One thousand and one nights old

No, I thought.

Species: Poltergeist

The shy boy in the hall with orange eyes. *The boy who should have known beetlbies didn't live in the bogs.* The stuttering boy who stood up for himself. *The boy who sat in the back to avoid the mirror.*

The boy who wasn't present at the ceremony.

The boy who deceived me.

The boy who tried to kill me.

"No..." I didn't know if I was saying that because I didn't want it to be him or if I was scolding myself for not realizing he had taken the form of an ogre this whole time. I had cared for him. Considered him a *friend*. "When... when did you find this?"

"I saw him leave his room an hour before the ball started. He isn't really the type to uh, pre-game, so… I don't know." He fiddled with his fingers as if he felt embarrassed by the reason.

"Don't silence yourself."

"I felt this hum inside of me, pulling me to follow him. He came here, and I went inside after he left, and then… then I found it." He pointed to the file creasing in my hand under my tight, shaking grip, afraid if I let go, he would slip away again.

Not this time.

Never again.

"I'm going to stop him," I pushed the file up against Dante's chest. "Now."

"You've become very bossy, my child," a voice aged like sweet-smelling poison said from the stairs. The lilt of *his* voice paralyzed every thought, each breath.

"Father?"

CHAPTER 33

He wore a blue coat that was too light for a moment like this.

Tailored too nicely for the money he sent back to Aunt Esther and me.

"Did you forget about my letter? I *always* keep my word," he regarded my formal attire with an amused gaze. "No matter the occasion."

"I—I—" The tip of a thought became sliced off before it could form. The only one that split through came in knife-like precision. "I expect your letter to arrive no later than the third week of October. If you fail to do so, I will come there and bring you home myself.

"I was so generous, too, sending your Headmaster away."

My brain stuttered.

"You," My father looked pointedly at Dante, then a fake smile bled across his face. "Would you be so kind as to give my daughter and me a moment?"

Dante met my gaze, eyes as uncertain as an overcast sky. I signaled the same feeling, but nodded that it was okay to go. The idea of him returning to a room with the Child of Mara made me swallow hard, but what frightened me most was that somehow, my father's presence felt more sinister.

At the sound of the door below shutting, my father sighed. "He's horribly chatty. Your Headmaster."

Tenold? Chatty? If anyone were to make you change every aspect of yourself, it would be Adam Seraphin. No matter how far away or too close for comfort he was, you would say or do anything to please him for a reason you weren't quite sure of.

"You should be grateful I was kind enough to take such a precaution."

"Precaution? Father, what are you talking about?" I rose to my feet. Even though I was only a few inches shorter, it unnerved me to stand before him.

"See, I knew I was right. He raved about how intelligent you are, but if that were true, you would have left Esalroth already," he tutted. Words piled in my throat, but I dared not speak them. Despite having done nothing but change and grow since I stepped through the gates of Esalroth, the sight of him, our grey eyes, our similar nose, reminded me I was nothing but *his* little girl.

"Though, I am flattered you thought your 'stutter worthy' power came from me."

The power of the one will make all stutter.

"But m-mom…," I warbled. "She was a witch. L-like Aunt Esther."

His pasty face steamed red. "DON'T YOU DARE COMPARE MY SISTER TO HER!" He roared.

I cowered back. The soft fabric of my dress grew moist, shrinking around me. He inhaled and returned his hollow smile as though it had never left.

"I'm going to tell you a story from the lips of Mara herself," he smiled. I wanted nothing more than to run. I had heard enough of Mara and her wicked heir. *He* was keeping me from ending them, leaving both of them to only ever be spoken of again in stories with unhappy ends. The fear that if I blinked, his grin would widen and consume me whole stopped me from protesting.

"Mara was born with the sole purpose to wreak havoc on the world. Nothing more. Nothing less. She terrorized anyone she felt like. The good. The bad. The best. As she was leaving one of her victims, a wizard started to heal them. Forgetting her centuries—*ions*—worth of torturing people, she wondered why she could not bring about the same grateful look the victim gave

the wizard. So, she did what she did best. She *lied*. She

transformed herself into a human woman and told the wizard a

fake name. She told him she was a witch and offered her help in

aiding people. Her beautiful form and charming words beguiled

the wizard and he fell in love with her. After Mara got what she

wanted—a child—she revealed her true self to the wizard. He cast

a protection spell, and Mara fled, but not before trying to steal the

baby… and the wizard's sister."

"No," I gasped. "No, that's not—"

It all aligned too perfectly.

"Thankfully, the wizard scared her off before his sister

fell for the trick. The demon escaped and fled to the Isle of Man.

However, the wizard had friends there. For saving the head of the

Tenold house from a ghastly disease, the family agreed to exorcise

Mara with their use of spà—Norse magic. It was a shame they all

died because of her, but the wizard kept his child and his sister

safe. He never let them leave the cottage."

He put his hand on my trembling shoulder. "Not just to

keep *them* safe, but to keep the world safe from the half-demon

child."

I wrenched away from his grasp. The floor pivoted out

from under me. The room began to sweat and shrink. The gears of

the clock screeched as they pierced my mind. "That's not

possible. I—I can't shapeshift. The Child of Mara—"

"Would only be able to either shapeshift or alter their powers." He put a jeweled finger to his chin. "It seems like you got the latter gene." All this time, I thought my power was transforming the feelings of others and myself and manipulating it into magic, but maybe that was just a means to *accessing* that magic. I was accelerating so fast in training. Was that just because I was only performing a fraction of what I was capable of?

No. I couldn't be the monster I had sought all this time. It wasn't just infallible. It was impossible.

"Then who hid Charlie's file? Who committed all those attacks?"

"Still him, so, I suppose you did solve *one* thing correctly." His congratulatory smile only made me recoil in horror further. "But don't worry, my child. I've already spoken with the poltergeist. Thankfully, he wasn't trying to hurt you, just the Headmaster. He seemed awfully regretful about hurting that moth…" He pondered on the tragedy for a snap second and tossed it away as if it was just a means to an end. "He was smart, though. I'll give him that. Stealing his file, knowing how suspicious he looks. It all works quite well for us, though."

Everything in me had gone numb. My muscles, my thoughts, my memories. There was no truth to me but being a scared child in the clocktower.

He placed his hand on my shoulder again, firmer. A horrid attempt at caring. He never did have practice at paternity. "Don't worry, my child," he repeated. The depth of his blue eyes was as thin as ice. As harmless as the moment before it cracks and swallows you whole. "You will not be... found out. The poltergeist is being taken care of right now."

Shouts and hollers erupted from the courtyard below. I ran over to the clock, searching for the latch to open the space between the six and seven hands.

"What are you doing?" My father hissed.

"I can't let him take the fall for this." I patted down the reverse imprint of the clock, moonlight starting to stream through it.

"He has hurt people, Blythe. He is not innocent."

"Neither am I! He lashed out because he knew he would be to blame. They suspected the ogre rather than blonde human Blythe even though it has been *me* they're after. They will kill him, father!"

"Do not take that tone with me, young lady!" He shouted, pointing a finger. "You will do as I tell you. I am your father."

"And Aunt Esther is your sister. That didn't stop you from pushing the responsibility of raising me onto her. That didn't stop you from lying to her about..." Mara. The devil's older sister. The reason children have nightmares. The physical personification of evil. "Mom."

THE SON OF MARA

He scoffed. "Esther can't handle the truth. She fell for Mara's deception."

Aunt Esther's words rang in my head. "She was raving about someone being after us—her, me, and you—and she told me we had to flee." My father.

That stale anger flexed its grasp. "If Mara was so deceitful... if her one true goal was to use you for a child, why didn't she leave right after she had me? Why did she leave only after she told you who she is?" I shot back. *Why go through the trouble of buying tickets to the ferry as a ruse?* She was an immortal demon. If she wanted to steal her baby, she could have killed my aunt with a snap of her fingers and left.

"All part of her act to torture us!" He was unravelling in a way I had never seen him. But then again, it had been a long time since I had seen him. "She *thrived* off of that, don't you understand? She was born to be a monster."

I pushed harder, and a triangle of the clock flung open. "Then what was I born to be, dad?"

The smile plastered across his face delved into a scowl, aggravated by the act of having to reveal his true feelings to get his way. "Hidden."

I would not let the last time my father saw me be in fear. I would not let him see how a single word carved the last shell of hope he would return to *be* my father, out of my heart. I held my head up before him and leapt from the clocktower, hoping the powers of being a half-demon would come through in time to catch me. I would rather shatter my spine than stay with Adam Seraphin any longer.

I slowed my fall, using the fear throttling through me as a cushion. For the first time, no one so much as gave me a glance as I landed.

Too much chaos was ensuing.

The golden lanterns hanging from the walls spilled over the courtyard in sandy shades, making it look like a gladiator arena. The wind swept in leaves off the roof, occasionally landing on the people in elegant dress wear, roaring and hollering at something near the edge of the woods.

Charlie.

I pushed through the crowd of raging students. Some had already summoned their powers or bared their claws as if they were about to hurt him. Not if. *When.*

I moved quicker.

Finally, I came to the head of the mob. Tenold had cornered Charlie by standing in front of the paths to the woods, leaving him caught in between the crowd and the Norse practitioner weaponing the staff he had saved for over a decade.

That had been harnessing power for over a decade.

But he wasn't the cowering boy in class. He was *enraged*. He cradled a ball of fire in one hand and twirled three rocks the size of a fist in the other, exposing his fangs as he stood in a fighting stance.

At one thousand and one nights old, he refused to let teenagers be the death of him.

"Stop! Stop this!" I yelled, placing myself between Charlie and the crowd. The fire in his palms dulled but did not dissipate.

"KILL HIM, BLYTHE!" Someone shouted. The crowd whooped in hungry agreement.

"FULFILL THE PROPHECY!" Another hollered.

"NO!" I shouted back. "Killing him is not the answer to solving this! He is your friend! He is my friend!"

"HE ALMOST KILLED CLYDE!" A voice I recognized to be Gus' blared.

"He meant to hurt me!" I lied, knowing that his intention to hurt the Headmaster would enrage them further. "If anyone should be angry at him it's me and me alone!"

"FINE!" A husky voice declared. Taking off his silk grey suit jacket, Bayle stood out from the crowd, shooting his hands ablaze. "I'll finish this."

It was too late. I couldn't save us both.

"HE IS NOT THE SON OF MARA!" I bellowed.

Bayle stopped.

This was it. This was the end. I felt everything I had ever wanted slip from my grasp with the gasps of the crowd. The way Dante traced his fingers. His thoughtfulness. The way Clyde glowed at just the sight of her friends. Her generosity. The way Gus would do anything for those he loved. His loyalty. Even Melsella and the way she cared so deeply, but so silently.

I watched my words ripple through the crowd like a tsunami. "I am Blythe Seraphin, and I am the Son of Mara!"

The crowd went as still as death. I felt the fire in Charlie's palms extinguish. I heard the clink of Tenold's staff hitting the ground.

The eyes that had gawked at me with admiration, idolization, evaporated. Rage, betrayal, *hatred* seeped out of them as if that was the only feeling ever there to begin with. One pair of eyes stood out from the rest. Professor Norwood's weren't petrified or alarmed. They were solemn and pitiful. Like she had suspected it all along but wished it would never have come to this.

"I have only just found out," I tried to explain. "I had every intention of—"

"YOU LIED TO US!" Bayle boomed. The same accusation Adam smeared across my mother. The crowd stirred.

"DEMON!" Someone called.

"SNEAK!"

Bayle aimed his arms towards me. "I was right," he said so low I almost didn't hear him. A disturbed smile distorted his usually aloof face. "I WAS RIGHT!" He laughed maniacally, hysterically. "I AM THE CHOSEN ONE!" He shouted, drunk on the idea.

"GET THAT DEMON!" A student cried.

"GET HER, BAYLE."

Instinctively, I turned to the only authority figure, stupidly thinking that since he was an adult, he would correct them.

Instead, Headmaster Christer Tenold said in his bored way of speaking, "You heard them, Mr. Bayle."

I felt a wave of heat streak closer to me as I whipped around. Charlie shoved me out of the way, sending us toppling in opposite directions. Bayle may as well have been rabid as he turned to Charlie.

"YOU CAN'T STOP ME!" He barked at him, his fist growing molten as he slammed it into Charlie's chest.

"NO!" I shouted, raising my arm and knocking Bayle back into the column with the force of my fear—a second too late.

Charlie choked on the pain—the *blood*—as I scampered over to him. Bayle's fist had melted the surface of his skin, his bones, and plunged fire straight into his heart.

No. He was okay. He was a poltergeist. This was just a form. He would be okay. It would require deep magic to kill him.

A slow clink of a staff approaching sounded against the stone. The Headmaster towered above me, face unfazed by the blood gushing from Charlie. His student.

"Are you associated with the demon, poltergeist?" He asked.

"No. He's not. He—" I started.

Blood spattered out of his mouth as Charlie spoke, staining the white of his fangs. "We both call hell home, s-so I suppose so. D-don't worry, Headmaster. We'll save you a seat."

It all happened too fast. A second at most. Like this was as ordinary a task as filing paperwork to the Headmaster. A task he had practiced. Had waited for.

He pointed his staff at Charlie's face and uttered, "Framkvæmd."

I didn't know what the word meant. I didn't need to because Charlie stilled in my arms.

It was an exorcism.

"No, no, no, no," I cried. But it was done. The sunset orange of his eyes had set. The sage of his skin had faded to a color too artificial to be claimed by nature. Too fresh to be associated with death. "Please, Charlie, hold on." I clutched his hand in mine, begging my blood to go help him instead. "We're friends, right? Friends stick together, so stay with me," I pleaded. "Do you hear me? Stay! Don't shy away! Fight!" He laid there.

Still.

I wiped a tear from my eye, and pressed my hand to the cavity in his chest. "It's okay. You're okay. I'm going to fix this," The warmth in his blood slipped with every sorry attempt at stopping the bleeding. "I'm going to… "

Save him?

The idea I was a savior was so deeply ingrained in my psyche that I had done the same thing these people had done to me. I overlooked that my friends were a vampire, a human moth, a summoner, a *poltergeist*. They didn't need my saving, and without me, they probably would still be intact—or here at all.

Charlie's form started to wither into ash—like all exorcised creatures, unable to even have a burial.

Who would mourn a demon?

The crowd shuffled closer to get a look at Charlie, who was reduced to nothing but a mound of gray flakes as if he was nothing more than wood for kindling. Not a classmate. Not a friend. I watched as the sudden sweep of a fall breeze carried him away. The only piece of him that remained was his jacket, left unwhole without its owner.

My peers looked down at my hands, coated in the stray ash from me holding him. The set of their eyes weren't concerned like with Clyde but intrigued.

Relieved.

Rage boiled the tears rising in me, evaporating them with a snap.

They told me I was destined to save them. They told my mother the only thing she could be was a monster.

They were the liars.

They took the lives of two people who couldn't even give their last words.

And for their crimes, I would show them a true, vengeful monster.

I rounded on Tenold. A phantom of red thorned from my palms, coiling itself around his neck. He clawed at it, but it wasn't something for him to touch. His staff slipped from his grasp. I held him above the trees, his feet dangling, and his eyes bulging. The wrath of sixteen years—the age of the prophecy—no, centuries unwound inside me.

I hurled him into the woods.

Bayle stood up from his sprawled position against the column I had thrown him into, rubbing his head. He ignited his hands.

"You want to go again now?" I laughed, feeling drunk on the agony, the pain, the *wrath*. "Okay."

THE SON OF MARA

He blew on his hands and a rocket of fire roared towards me. I twisted my hands and the flames curled into my control, the light flooding the courtyard with an enraged orange. I pushed them back at him. and he ran behind the same column for cover.

"Oh, come on!" I hollered. "YOU'RE TOO EASY!" He jumped back out, growling as he smashed his hands into the ground. Veins of fire cracked through the stone, racing towards my feet. I twirled my finger, and the water from the fountain spiraled out and spilled over the floor, making the cobblestone hiss.

What was it he called me? A lovely meal?

Now who looked like a lamb?

I sent threads of crimson up his ankles, up to his torso, and forced his hands up.

I flung him into the clock tower. Maybe he would have the pleasure of meeting Adam. I was sure they had a lot in common.

Wisps of red magic unfurled from my chest. My mother's power. The spirit I had felt within me all along was finally unbound from the demands and constraints of a father's will, a prophecy's words.

Slowly, mythical students stepped in front of the crowd, ravenous for their chance to prove themselves.

To be the one.

I laughed.

How funny they were.

A water nymph lunged forward, spurting water at me. I snatched it in mid-air, contorting it into a sphere until it ensnared her with my fury. Vines burst from the ground and wrapped around my ankles. A forest sprite extended his arm, sending a thorny stem straight for my head. I stretched my fingers and the vines shriveled into a black corpse. I tore the vines from my legs and sent them snaking around him until he struggled against his own magic.

Where is the one now? I chuckled.

Stomps shook the walls. I whipped my head up as a minotaur bulleted down from the top of the courtyard, only a foot or two from impact. A flash of black caught hold of his neck, driving him to the ground.

Dante.

He rocked the minotaur with punches that reverberated off of him. Dante had always been so docile I forgot he possessed raw vampire strength and agility.

"You…" Helped me. The demon. The monster we had sought all this time. "My mom. She's the reason…" I couldn't bring myself to finish the sentence.

He pushed the hair back from his eyes, unchanged as midnight. "I didn't know your mom. I only know you."

THE SON OF MARA

I shook my head, allowing the words to rip from my throat like a bandage over a fresh wound. "I can't risk hurting you."

He stood up, stepping towards me. He moved like how I imagined the chords of a piano would. "The sun is also a star, Blythe," he said. His occasionally awkward, borderline cryptic way of speaking clicked into a language I understood better than my first. The hate surging through my veins felt as foreign as a blood type that didn't match.

It wasn't mine.

The mob—even beyond the crowd—it was *theirs*.

The ions of disdain for my mother, for me. The horror stories. The names. The lies.

They belonged to them. Not me.

The sun is also a star. I didn't have to burn them up. I didn't have to scorch them. Scorn them.

I could be the freckles of night. The gleam in a river of midnight. The ball of power that could wipe out the entire planet but chooses to be a mere speck in our sky so the evening may not be as scary.

"Then you are the night I shine in," I replied.

He bowed his head, unable to look me in the eyes as the vulnerability he hadn't let himself bare in a very long time rippled from his heart to mine. "I will follow you whenever you rise and whenever you set."

I looked at the crowd. *This* was all I ever needed. To be seen for who I am. Not the sheltered witch in a cottage, tamed by my aunt's misguidance. Not "the one", forced to dress and act by the rigid standards of decades gone by. I was no longer parading around as something I was not. I was Blythe Seraphin, daughter of Mara. Niece of Esther Seraphin. And I would wilt no further under the unearned expectations of others.

I would enact my mother's wrath by showing everyone *who* I was.

I was the Son of Mara.

And what that meant was entirely up to me.

The crowd parted as Bayle, shredded and enraged, stumbled forward with emblazoned hands. The brown of his eyes had become unhinged. I flung Dante to the side as Bayle hurled a flurry of fire at me. I redirected it into the sky, and it fumed into the night as if a dragon had just spewed it. He whipped a blade of flames towards me, and I forced them down to the ground, singing the cobblestone.

"YOU CAN'T DEFEAT ME, MONSTER!" He blared, spit flying from his mouth. *Monster.* My mother, Dante, Gus, Charlie, and now me.

The name was starting to form a new meaning with such good company.

THE SON OF MARA

I took a step towards him and my knees buckled as a haze blurred my vision. All the power I had just expended was finally collecting its due. I narrowly dodged the blades of fire— what appeared to be fire—that sliced through the air. I ducked as I felt a ball of heat rocket overhead and into the wall behind me. My ribs felt as if they were

closing in

on

themselves.

It.

Feels. So.

       Heavy.

My eyes. Do.

My head.   *F u zzzzz y.*

My stomach.

So empty.

He savored crossing the space, getting closer to me. I crawled away as much as my body would allow. "I just want you to know this, demon. I never wanted you. I could never want something like *you*." He turned the last word over on his tongue like it was sour. "I figured if I couldn't be the one, I would get as close to that power as I could." He shrugged. "I won't doubt myself again."

His words intertwined with the memories I was struggling to cope with—the past that was so vivid it personified itself physically.

My back hit the wall, and the stench of burnt vines pulled back the darkness inching over my vision.

A sharp acidity accented the smell.

I looked behind me at the charred leaves I was crushing.

Junifere leaf.

Maybe, since I was only *half*-demon, practicing witchcraft was still a necessity to maintain my health. As my stomach and mind threatened to swap places, I patted the deck of cards in my boot. I had grown so accustomed to their presence, I never thought to take them out.

I tore off a handful of leaves as I silently apologized and thanked them. I pulled out a card. The Queen of Hearts turned her nose up.

Seems fitting.

THE SON OF MARA

I licked the card to ensure the junifere would stick and sprinkled some on. Bayle raced towards me. I ran left, leading him towards the fountain.

"DON'T RUN FROM ME!" He boomed.

I stopped at the edge of the fountain, holding the card over the water with one hand. "I never will again."

I blew the junifere in my other hand into his face and dropped the card in the water. He tried to swat it off, unaware that would only help the process I was silently asking the goddesses, Aunt Esther, and my mom to assist in.

I clapped once.

Water splashed the back of my dress as a card appeared at the height of where Bayle had stood, gliding to the ground. In the fountain, Bayle was staring at his useless hands, too drenched to produce a single spark.

I breathed in the cool air, smelling of herbs and cobblestone, and it solidified my muscles, snuggled in my stomach, and found shelter in my spirit.

"A good witch is a prepared witch."

The feeling of weaving my two halves together felt as strange and as beautiful as rain in the sunlight.

I drew a circle with my finger and red rope curled around Bayle. I raised him to my height as I stepped closer. His suit had turned the darkest shade of grey while water dripped off of his scowling, bitter face.

"I can feel the ambition you cradle, like it may burn you if you do not fulfill it. Do not let me be here when it consumes you." I dropped him back down and allowed my words to finish him.

I felt Dante's eyes widen in a thick horror. "BLYTHE, WATCH OUT!" He pointed behind me. Headmaster Christer Tenold had returned from the woods, crumpled leaves and twigs disrupting the pure white of his hair. His eyes were hungry, ravenous.

Tired.

Spools of green light zapped from his staff. I redirected them with a swish of a hand, allowing the walls to crumble instead of me. But he kept advancing. His magic pushed hard against mine. Ancient, unhealed, *lonely* hatred sizzled my palm as he moved closer until he was only a few feet away.

"You're the reason they're all dead, don't you understand?" He said, only letting his voice crack the littlest bit at the end.

"Adam Seraphin misled them. My mother only wanted a better life for herself and me," I pushed.

"That doesn't undo all the pain, the *blood* she spilled over centuries!" His voice lurched, scraping my ears in its anger. He fired another spell at me, which I thrust to the side.

THE SON OF MARA

"I know," The red in my hands faded. My palms remembered the tenderness of Dante coming to accept his past. Even as a child, he chose the harder choice. The one best for the world. "But, I can start."

I closed my eyes as Tenold aimed his staff at me. Vibrant green from the simple carved wood pulsated even behind my closed lids.

I hoped my mom would be proud.

Suddenly, a blast of wind blew my hair over my face, whooshing into my ears like a tornado. Tenold flew from his feet and hurtled into the wall. His staff fell to the ground, and creatures half the size of my finger inched over it. Their white masses started nibbling away at the wood, chipping it down to a toothpick in mere seconds. The carpenter of Lucifer's favorite insect: *terminationmites*.

From the opposite side, Melsella stood beside Gus with her arms raised. "I don't think my parents would care very much about a murderer's opinion of me!" Melsella chimed, scrunching her grey brows. Clyde looped her arm through Melsella's.

Gus walked over and crouched down beside the knocked out body of the Headmaster. He took off his mask to reveal his eyes, plucked with tears. His lip wobbled even as he strained to maintain a hardened face. "You—you—" He sniffled, unable to deliver his damnation.

Dante placed a hand on Gus' shoulder, helping him to his feet. Shaking his head, Dante said, "You've been so brave already."

Gus' brown eyes—as fresh as bakery chocolate—melted as they looked up at Dante. He stood at only about his waist. Suddenly, Gus buried his face in Dante's black button up, wrapping him in a hug. Dante looked baffled, but instantly melted into it, embracing him back. Gus poked his head out from Dante's jacket, rolling his eyes as he ushered me in.

There is never just one star in the sky. There are constellations.

CHAPTER 34

The trees planted in the front of Esalroth bloomed into cherry blossoms in the spring. To the gate's resentment, dandelions were insistent on growing in the nooks of stone leading up to the academy. Dante plucked one, and it handed to me, turning to the side again to wait. I nodded to the past, then planted a kiss on his cheek, the top of my head brushing under his black floppy brim hat.

I didn't kiss him to prove anything. I didn't need to. He knew. I knew. I did it because I wanted to. Because he is Dante and I am Blythe. That was all.

In his head to toe, shoulder to wrist, all black attire, I could see the sweat beading on his forehead. Dante. Cold Dante. I suspected nerves were behind it. As if nature itself heard his silent pleas, a cool breeze rushed all around us.

"I'll have to send a tornado to cool you down if you keep wearing things like that," Melsella said, coming up from behind us. She crossed her arms and turned her face away as she continued. "I have more than enough parasols that would suffice in keeping you shaded." I sensed her stomach grow staticky.

It was the first time I felt Melsella nervous.

Dante placed a hand on her shoulder, and her eyes went wide. "Thank you. That would be helpful."

She smiled as she sputtered, "Nothing—no problem is—no problem at all."

Clyde flew through the front doors with Melsella's wings strapped to her feet. "Headmaster Norwood is coming! She's coming!" She squeaked.

Melsella squeezed her hand in shared joy while Gus pretended to not be equally as excited.

"Those," Gus said, pointing to the dandelion in my hand. "Are weeds."

"They're also edible," Aunt—I mean—*Professor* Seraphin replied from behind us. She would know, after all, being the professor of Esalroth's newest class: magical healing.

"Make way, stories of old!" Headmaster Norwood called, hauling the new plaque outside. After the council found attacking a student to be distasteful to their image, the most worthy choice filled the position of Headmaster.

THE SON OF MARA

I looped my arm in Dante's, and he smiled wide, his fangs glinting in the afternoon sun. The crowd followed her eagerly out through the gates.

"Would you do the honors, Mr. Shyung?" She asked.

Blushing at being called upon, he ripped the old sign off the stone column supporting the gates, tossing it on the ground. Gus gave it a kick (for good measure).

Norwood nailed the new plaque into place, cementing the changes from the year with the taps of her hammer. Some people still glared at me or scooted away if I walked too close, but standing beside me were people who would send a hurricane or a rabid canine at those who dared to brush past me a little too forcefully. People who would wipe my tears with their own sleeve and fashion me a dress just because. A person who, one day, promised to travel the world with me, stopping wherever an Inferno could illuminate book pages as well as minds. Unbeknownst to him, he would be the most exciting and beautiful sight himself, no matter where we went.

And, I had my mother. Not in the traditional sense, but I saw her in the red of my magic. The hazel of my aunt's eyes. The gold in a life directed by my own choices. My *own* expectations.

I didn't need more than that.

A boy with a hidden talent for comebacks should be here too, but I was sure Professor Thrall was appreciating his help locating the crawdads. I kept his jacket hanging on the banister of my bed. Sometimes it would go missing when it got too cold on the sea.

Students clapped as the final nail held in the stone. Words carved in the gold of this new world gleamed: *Esalroth Academy of the Mythical, Magical, and Magnificent.*

ACKNOWLEDGEMENTS

This book would not exist without my mom, who allowed me to spend my summer writing (instead of doing whatever a teenager should do) because writing makes me happy. That was the only reason she needed. Thank you, mom, for your endless, enthusiastic support for even my littlest of achievements.

Thank you to my family, especially my Nana and Poppy, for reading the first drafts, and just for asking me how the process was going. It was nice to know someone else cared.

Thank you to the editor of this novel, Erin Bledsoe, who gave my characters the love they needed, and most importantly— fixed my commas.

Thank you to my friends for answering questions that can basically be summed up as: "how do people react?"

Finally, thank *you*. Thank you for picking up this book, whether you were one of the first readers who took a chance on a self-published teenager, or someone later on who heard some nice things about it and figured, why not? I hope you know these characters are yours as much as they are mine. They can be your friends, your family, just as they will always be mine. Esalroth belongs to all the people who feel misplaced. After all, it is a home for the Mythical, Magical, and Magnificent.

What category you are in, well, that is entirely up to you.

~ Madison McMahon

MADISON MCMAHON was born and raised in New England as a fan of *Little Women* first, and an American second. She wrote her debut novel, *The Son of Mara*, the summer going into her junior year of high school because she absolutely detests the heat. Madison can still be found in a small city in New England where she plans on going to college for creative writing (or something of the sort).

Find more from Madison at
www.authormadisonmcmahon.com

Made in United States
North Haven, CT
16 October 2021